CALUMET CITY PUBLIC LIBRARY

3 1613 004

W9-CCN-683

NAPPILY ABOUT US

 # 7

Trisha R. Thomas

FACE PRESS
CALIFORNIA

CALUMET CITY PUBLIC LIBRARY

Nappily About Us

Copyright © 2011 by Trisha R. Thomas

This is a work of fiction. All of the characters, organizations, and events portrayed in this novel are either products of the author's imagination or are used fictitiously.

Nappily About US. Copyright 2011 by Trisha R. Thomas. All rights reserved. Printed in the United States of America. No part of this book may be used or reproduced in any manner whatsoever without express written permission. For information, address Facepress Publisher, info@facepresspublisher.com.

WWW.FACEPRESSPUBLISHER.COM

ISBN 978-0-9834560-1-8

AA
THO

6/13

11.99

Ing.

For my family who loves unconditionally

Also By Trisha R. Thomas

Nappily Ever After
Roadrunner
Would I Lie To You
Nappily Married
Nappily Faithful
Nappily In Bloom
Un-Nappily In Love

From The Top

Sirena Lassiter was nobody's video vixen. For the record, she only agreed to do a couple of scenes as a favor for K-Bee who was now a popular director. The shoot started six hours ago and all she'd done so far was bounce to the beat, sitting behind the steering wheel of a convertible Mercedes. The blue sheen of the car matched the lipstick she was wearing. She kept a fierce grip on the steering wheel, determined to ignore the gum-popping girl in her ear.

But suddenly the gum popping stopped. Sirena knew what was coming next. The girl's raspy voice cut through the music followed by a tap on her shoulder. "Oh my *godddd,* aren't you Sirena?"

The Prada shades covered enough of her face so the girl couldn't see her scowl. If one more un-trained hand touched, or nudged her to ask if she was indeed Sirena Lassiter they were going to lose a limb.

"Girl, what's up with you? Haven't heard from you in a minute. When's your next album droppin? I run Jam N Juice, the blog. So what, you're singing back-up on this joint?"

"I'm just doing a friend a favor," Sirena admitted. If it would end further conversation she would be grateful.

"Well let me know what's up. When you drop a new record, I'd love first dibs on an interview."

There was no new record. Sirena had nothing in the works so that wasn't happening. Her next project was postponed indefinitely because she hated every song sent her way. The producers from the record company were giving her all the slop while the good writing and beats were being kicked to the up-and-comers. It was the music execs way of making fast money. The new artist got paid peanuts and the music company would make millions. She knew exactly what they were up to, which was why she'd already planned her counter move. She needed JP. She called him Jay from the first day they'd met when she was eighteen. The two of them together had always meant magic.

Only problem was getting him to go along with the program. After the stunt she pulled last year, they hadn't seen or spoken more than three words to each other. How is Christopher? And even then, what she really meant was, have you forgiven me yet?

"Okay, CiCi, you're up." K-Bee snapped his finger and did a thumb thing.

"Did you just snap your finger at me, Kelvin Boggle the third," she enunciated. Announcing his real name in public was like a slap in the face. She'd known him when he was a mere errand boy for Hands Down records. Seemed these days he'd forgotten where he started. "I am not one of these…" she felt the glare of her unwanted comrades in scantily dressed clothing and lowered her voice. "I think you need to check yourself, okay. I'm here doing you a favor."

"A favor? I think it's mutual. CiCi, ain't nobody seen you in like a year, they might not even recognize you in this scene. Lets do this. All right. Time is money." He snapped his fingers again. The music cued. "All I need you to do is step out of the car, stroll to this point. Give that sexy smile and a wink. Joe will move toward you. Give him a sweet peck on the lips, and you earned yourself a cool five grand."

She took a few steps, tossed her shiny bronze hair over her shoulder and suffered through the rappers hands sliding up and down her waist. When he leaned in she turned her face and gave him the cheek.

"Cut. Whathahell?" Kelvin moved to Sirena. "Smack on the lips ain't gone kill you."

"Says you. I don't know where his foul mouth has been. That fool is not putting his lips near mine. You couldn't pay me enough."

"I don't have time for this. You either do what I tell you to do or I'll get somebody who will."

"Yeah, do what you have to," she said calling his bluff. She may not have been in the spotlight for the past year but she still had the power to get attention. There wasn't a week that didn't go by that she wasn't featured on some-one's gossip site, foul or not. It was still media.

"Okay. Fine. Right here." He pointed to the left of her mouth. "I'll get the shot and make it look like he kissed you on the lips."

"Unh, unh. What would I look like letting him put his gold tooth filled mouth on me? No. Not gonna happen, Kelvin. You said this was going to be fifteen minutes of work. I've been sitting around here all damn day. You got one more take. You want to do this or not?"

Kelvin looked around, worried how much of their conversation was being heard. "I see why nobody wants to work with you anymore, CiCi," he said before stomping off like a kindergartner. "Let's go. Cue the music."

What he said hurt her feelings. It also made her more determined than ever to teach everyone a lesson who'd disrespected her over the past year. The road to redemption would be long and hard but well worth the trip. She had a list of folks who were going to be sorry they ever crossed her path.

From the moment the media found out about Christopher who wasn't her little brother after all, nothing had gone right. Trifling home wrecker. Mother of the Year. All the labels and headlines used against her affected record sales, endorsements, and movie offers. All because Jay hadn't gone along with the program. But it wasn't truly his fault.

If there was anyone to blame, it was Venus, his needy wife. She getting pregnant and using it to keep him hostage is what ended all negotiations. Jay, Sirena, and Christopher, a real family quickly became a pathetic dream right along with her image.

You can't have everything you want. She'd accepted that fact a long time ago, or at least in the past six months. But she couldn't help it. She still daydreamed of a completely new scenario, one of peace and happiness. Having to watch him on TV every week pretending to be happy only made her know it was time she stepped up and saved him from his grim life. Sometimes what a person wanted wasn't always good for them, she'd have to make him understand. It was time to set things in motion and let the chips fall where they may.

Nappily About Us

My name is Venus Johnston and I'm in love with Jake Parson. I said this out loud like a recovering addict about five times a day. Waking up with a camera in my face each and every morning required this affirmation, otherwise what was I doing, the center of a television reality show viewed by millions of people every week. I feared a sex tape was not too far off in our future seeing as how my husband had me wrapped around his little finger. I realized I loved him more, and more each day. Just the sight of him coming out of the shower with the towel wrapped around his muscular abs with his body moist made my toes curl.

So if anyone was to ask how I was talked into having a house filled with monster size studio lights–the soft filtered kind, if I was going to be on display I could at least look healthy and glowing. Mini microphone boxes were set in the corners of every room to record conversations. A six-person crew with free reign over every part of my house. I could only say love was my reason for living this way. I would do just about anything for Jake and our family. Almost...anything.

"Good morning, baby," Darcie enunciated with a clip-board in her hand and a headset. Clearly she was in charge. "And Jake will say..."

"Can you give us a minute?" Jake sat up where we'd been in the bed pretending to have just awakened. When in truth we'd been awake for hours. I'd already fed the twins, cooked Mya and Christopher pancakes, and was back in bed to act like the day had just begun.

"Okay, take five."

The cameraman gladly accepted the break and lowered the heavy equipment from his shoulder.

"I can't do lines. I'm not an actor. I thought a reality show was about reality. Why do we have scripts if it's supposed to be in real-time?" This was the most complex issue for me to understand. I cringed listening to my bad rendition of being myself. I couldn't get my head around the fact that our lives were being orchestrated every minute of the day.

"Do overs," Jake corrected me. "It's not a script. Repeating what you already said naturally, but this time they can capture it. Baby please, we've been over this. I have studio time scheduled in one hour. We've got to wrap this up."

And so we begin again. "Good morning, baby," I said, reaching out to give Jake a kiss.

Mya, our seven year old daughter, couldn't wait for her big entrance. Christopher, our eleven-year old going on forty, tried unsuccessfully to hide his disdain by wearing a big painful smile. The children have been cued to do what they'd already done hours earlier. Bursting into the room to interrupt what could've been a steamy love moment. Jake and I are full of disappointment since we haven't made a physical love connection in months. That part was true. Some of the faux reality was actually real.

But who had time. In addition to Mya and Christopher we now had four-month old twins. Thank goodness the babies were safely tucked away from this nonsense, monitored by Gema, our nanny, and luckily had no idea their mommy and daddy had sold their souls to turn a buck.

"Okay, that's perfect. We got it," Darcie announced. The tall bookish redhead with dimples the size of almonds offered a professional tone, but underneath she had a take no prisoner kind of vibe. If you needed a dose of reality, Darcie was the one to give it to you. "Next we'll need the scene getting Christopher off to his first day of school."

"I don't start school till Monday," Christopher responded, unafraid of Darcie and her clipboard.

"Yeah, but we're doing the school wardrobe drama today." She half smiled. "Is that okay with you?"

Christopher slumped. "Can I go back and play with my game?"

"You can play for thirty minutes until your piano teacher gets here."

"And then we film first-day-at-school." Darcie refuses to back down. "You may also want to dress the part." Christopher gave her the death glare. He had a definite aversion to females in power. I was hoping he grew out of it before dating age. He'd never find a mate thinking he was in charge.

Although Jake appeared naked beside me, he jumped up wearing his jeans, slips on the shirt his assistant tosses him and is fully dressed for his day. "See you later, babe."

I somehow got shorted in the assistant department. There's no one to hand me my robe. I pulled myself up on my elbows keeping the sheet to cover my bare chest.

The crew cleared out but I was still scared to get out of my bed. Afraid somewhere a hidden camera would capture my love jugs, as Jake called them. I had yet to lose the baby weight. Nursing was supposed to be a cure-all. I'd read that it used an extra thousand calories a day to produce milk. It might've worked if I didn't eat an extra 2000 calories a day to make up for it. I tried not to obsess about the extra weight. Jake certainly wasn't complaining. He almost got as excited as the twins right before nursing hour. Seeing my heavy breasts full, ripe, and ready to burst made him a horn toad. Of course it didn't help that I'd kept him at bay for months now.

At least I had on leggings. I straddled my breast with both arms before I got securely wrapped and tied in my robe.

"Yes?" I answered whoever had knocked on my door. I tried to lighten my annoyance by singing my words. This had become annoying in itself. I never trusted people who put that lilt on the end of everything as if they were starring in a Disney movie.

"There's someone at the door. We need you to answer it so we can film." Shelly, the production assistant, had the second most horrible job. Most days I felt sorry for her more than for myself being the whipping girl to Darcie and her motley crew. *"Go get this, move that, don't just stand there."* I still held the top spot of having the worst job. I felt like Darcie was in charge of my life. Everyday I woke up wondering what she had in store for me, as if I was some puppet on a string.

"It's probably the piano teacher arriving early. Do you mind having someone get the door, please?"

She mumbled something, probably in her walkie talkie. "Darcie said we need for you to answer the door, now."

"But...fine. Okay. Just need to get dressed. I'll be right down." What I really want to do is climb down the trellis, jump in my car and drive far, far away. I was exhausted. Plum tired. The only way to explain why I'd signed on for this was to blame it on my condition. I was a love addict. I'd accepted this fact long ago. I needed to be the apple of someone's eye. To accomplish this complicated task you must be able to keep those apples in the air at all times, exemplify beauty, stamina and grace all at the same time. It was a terrible thing I'd done, pretending to be exactly who my husband had married six years earlier. Strong, determined, and willing to go the extra mile. Almost like being hired for a great job, only to wait for that knock on the door where the company tells you they made a mistake.

Except there's no recovery going on anytime soon. I married the man who made my world complete. If that world included a reality show where we had to discuss just about every detail of our private lives on camera, so be it.

Jake had a couple of successful movies under his belt as an actor. Before that he'd had a successful urban clothing company based on his popularity as a hip-hop artist in the late nineties. He'd produced and recorded hit songs for a number of other artists as well. He was no stranger on the billboard chart. He'd even been in the covers of magazines in the ads for Calvin Klein showing off his tight abs and amazing chest. For a while we were spilling with good fortune. Then a year passed and not one serious opportunity. Making a ton of money is only half the battle. The other task was keeping it. We had a huge house to maintain, children, nannies, housekeepers, and a nasty tax bill that had to be settled. What was left in the kitty would only last for so long.

Distinguished Gentleman was Keisha's brainchild. As Jake's manager, it was her job to make sure no one ever said, "Who's JP" again. The pitch was about his daily life, Jake as a real live hero in action, super dad, sex symbol, and keeper of the peace, all in a day's work. Drama wasn't something we were short on, so we figured it would be easy.

The hard part was pretending it didn't bother us having our lives fully exposed. Jake had always been a very private person even with his celebrity status. But then Sirena Lassiter came into the picture. She was a superstar in her own right. Their past life had produced a son, Christopher. She'd kept him under wraps by saying he was her little brother. Not even Jake had known he had a son. The news broke, and no one could stop talking about the scheming manipulation of Sirena Lassiter, pretending all these years that the boy was her little brother instead of her son.

Sirena Lassiter made it clear she wasn't mother material, especially if that meant she and Jake couldn't raise Christopher together. She'd rather wash her hands of the entire situation. Jake gladly took her up on the offer and made it official with a legal adoption. I would definitely say it was her loss and our gain.

If it hadn't been for Christopher, I don't think I would've gotten pregnant. A classic case of once you believe you have what you want, you actually get it. Jake and I wanted a son. We'd lost our baby to a stillbirth. It nearly broke our marriage apart. When Christopher showed up in our lives out of the blue, that chapter seemed to close. It seemed to settle our argument with God, and each other.

You Rang

Less than three minutes later, I was downstairs waiting for Darcie's silent finger count; four, three, two...

"Hello." Never in a million years would I have opened the door to a stranger if I had been home alone. Man, woman, or child, I would've simply stared at them through the peephole until they went away. Jake had die-hard fans that were capable of just about anything to be close to him, even getting past the security gate. "Can I help you?" I said to the woman wearing sunglasses bigger than her face. She looks to be thirty-something. Early thirties or younger I'm guessing because she's wearing a nose ring. Anyone close to my age was averse to unnecessary pain.

She looked harmless, but then again, they always do. Maybe the tutor had a replacement. She could also be a journalist or one of those bloggers who made a name for themselves by reporting what the traditional news wished they could without being sued.

"My name is Bliss."

Maybe in her twenties with that name.

She took off her sunglasses and locked eyes as if searching for recognition. "You're even prettier in person."

"Oh, thank you." I'm disarmed by her flattery. I haven't felt pretty since my third month of pregnancy with the twins. After that I ballooned to double my normal weight and only twenty of that belonged to the babies. Jake and I had been trying to get pregnant by any means necessary, including unpredictable fertility drugs, and monitoring ovulation like the stock market ticker every minute of the day. When we finally conceived, I wanted to be careful and make sure nothing went wrong, and went about becoming a human incubator. I ate, slept, ate, and exercised very lightly but mostly ate and slept.

Just the thought of my miracle babies and I could fill my breast filling up with that familiar tingling. I tapped an impatient finger on the open door. Time was running short. So I asked again. "Can I help you with something?"

"I know this may come as a shock to you, but I'm your sister. Henry Johnston is my father."

I turned to Darcie after closing the door. "Okay. Not in the mood. Why am I talking to a crazy person? Is this your doing?" I made the cut across the air, signaling camera off, which was the accepted sign to stop filming. However, the camera was still running, still pointed at me. I reached around my waist under my shirt and powered off the microphone. The tape would be no good without sound. The doorbell rang again. I flapped my hands like a bird. "I'm being set up, right? Why would you send this crazy lady to my door?"

"I did not. No. Absolutely not," Darcie responded un-convincingly.

Maybe it wasn't her doing. She knew my history for-wards and back. Raised in suburbia. One brother, no sisters, a loving two-parent household. Sending someone to my door claiming to be my sister was reaching way out the realm of reality. The bell rang a second time, then a third, chiming through the house like high noon at church. I'm guessing the woman used that sister line to get past security. "I'm calling the police."

Darcie was on my heels. "Have you considered that she might be telling the truth?"

I was already half way up the stairs. "How? Not possible. She's younger than me, and my mom and dad are still married." I give her my *duh* expression.

Underneath her pink rimmed glasses Darcie gave me a *yeah-and* scowl right back. "I think you should at least talk to her. If she's crazy all the better. Makes for good television. And honestly, this week has been a real snooze fest. We need something popping," she said with a finger snap that seemed odd coming from a white girl.

****

Henry and Lauren were born on December 5th, three days before my own birthday. I had a C-section. I wasn't going to survive pushing two humans out to the world the old fashioned way. I held Henry first. Lauren came a few short seconds later. I named them after my father and Jake's mother. I gave Lauren my mother's middle name, Pauletta to quail any jealousy.

Our lovely innocent specimens were going to be our last chance at redemption, at doing something good and completely infallible. A son and a daughter, a gift so wonderful I got teary eyed with gratefulness.

I smiled down at Lauren. She smiled back, happy for a full belly and the loving arms holding her. Her eyes also told me to get on with my life. *I won't be a kid forever and you're going to need something besides me, and my bro to fulfill you.* But I can't think of anything better to do besides taking care of them, at least for now.

When she's full, she always pulls away from my nipple and gives me a few seconds to pull her up to be burped or there will be hell to pay. Her scream can call down thunder. After a good solid belch, I hand her over to Gema. She hands me the next loving customer.

Henry always patient and accepting keeps his fuss to a minimum. They each have their preferred side. I hold Henry on the left. I'd gotten in the habit of feeding him last. I'm hoping there will be no psychological repercussions, but it's naturally a better fit. By the time it's his turn to nurse, my left breast has expanded to the size of a bowling ball. Henry's appetite is of a growing boy so nothing gets left behind. He has Jake's kind caring eyes. He blinks sweetly before closing his eyes and getting down to business.

The gentle knock at the door was the dreaded signal I didn't want to hear. News about the crazy lady downstairs. Darcie promised to vet her, find out whether she'd been institutionalized locally, or flew here from a distance.

"I think you're going to want to hear this," Darcie said approaching me with her mini cam.

"I'm almost through. Can it wait five more minutes?" Holding my babies brought me joy. Sometimes I felt like I was going to spill over with too much emotion. I'd been waiting for the hormones to level out. Crying when happy had to be the ultimate sign of insanity. Yet, it's what happened sometimes when I held them, inhaling their goodness, grateful beyond measure.I swiped my eyes. I kissed Henry before handing him over to Gema who had already put a fresh diaper on Lauren. I wasn't too keen on having a nanny at first. I'd experienced one before and was badly scarred. No one should have that much power over you. This time I hired one after a long interview process. Gema Gerwinski won out over twenty candidates, all sent from an agency that did more security background checks than the FBI. I trusted her with my babies. She loved them as if they were her own.

Darcie sat beside me while I put my deflated breasts away. She pushed play.

"*My mother died. She didn't want me to feel like I had no one left after she was gone. She wanted me to contact Venus and my brother Timothy. Henry Johnston is our father. Millicent Gray is my mother. This is the picture I have of them, the only one my mother had. She gave it to me. They look so in love. But what do you do? He was married and had two other children. I'm sorry to have put all of this all in the open. But I have a brother and a sister...and a father that I'd like to get acquainted with. I couldn't wait for a good time, there was no good time.*" I pushed the Stop button.

I'm not sure what to say. My mouth has gone dry. "This doesn't prove anything. Trust me, I've seen some coo-coo's in my day and she's one of them."

"There's an easy way to find out. You can ask your father if he knows this woman, Millicent."

"I could. But I'm not. So you'll have to figure out something else to fill our time slot."

"Well, you're going to have to come at least speak to her. She said she's not leaving until you do."

"Oh really. Okay, we'll see about that."

"If you call the police, we have a right to film that too. It's in the contract," Darcie said matter-of-factly. The contract of which she's referring is about fifty pages long with every page ending with a threat of being sued for breach of said contract. They have a right to film between the hours of 8am to 10pm. If my imaginary sister would've shown up after bath hour, this all could've been worked out privately.

Darcie handed me a printout. "Listen, I already had the legal department for the production company run a background check. I had it faxed so you could see for yourself. She's not a criminal or a professional stalker. She just might be your sister and you're throwing away an opportunity to get to know her."

I took the paper and scanned as much as possible without looking too interested. Place of birth. She was born in Los Angeles too. As if that meant anything. Birthdate. I would've been seven when she was born. I handed it back. "I need to think about it."

"There's a woman downstairs who says she's my sister," I announced to Jake on the phone. He hated to be interrupted during studio time though he was no more than a few steps away. He had the home studio built when we'd first bought the house. He's currently working on an album, not his own, but as the producer of a young kid named, Gerald Frazier, aka, RikerIsland. Of all the stupid names... I'd asked Jake, "Does he know that's the name of a prison?"

"Too late," Jake had responded. "It's already tattooed on his arm." Thank goodness Jake had only one tattoo on his left bicep no bigger than a quarter. He said it was the most agonizing thirty minutes of his life and he'd never do it again. "You know there's always going to be people coming out of the woodwork," he said trying to calm me down. "You can't believe everything someone says. Sounds pretty suspect, if you ask me."

"That's what I said, but Darcie is convinced we need to have this conversation on film. She's convinced she's real. I halfway think she put her up to it. Apparently the past few days around here have been a snooze fest."

"Yeah, things have been pretty dead on my end too. We wrapped up two more songs. Overall, nothing to report home about." He paused long enough for me to know what's coming. "Just do it, babe. Talk to the woman. Feel her out. If there's no truth to it, send her packing."

"My father would never have had an affair on my mother. Not in a billion, gazillion, years. He wouldn't be alive now if he did. You know my mother did not play. She ran her ship high and tight. There would've been no room for error. Least of all my dad's error."

After a long pause, Jake said, "We all make mistakes."

I stayed quiet for fear I would ask, what kind of mistakes *do we* all make? I'm not up for any of his latest confessions so I shifted my attention back to the subject at hand.

"My father wouldn't make that kind of mistake. He's a better man than that. Are you coming to handle this, or should I?"

"I'm sure you can handle it. I can't walk out of here without finishing this set. Just put on your diplomatic hat. Give the woman ten minutes and put her out the door."

"Fine." I said before hanging up the phone. Something in my gut told me to just say 'no'. I wanted to tell Darcie to get that woman out of my house so I wouldn't even have to look at her. But then I remembered, it was all about the drama. The never ending need to have a story to tell. The crew needed to film at least sixty hours of usable footage. I'd end the snooze fest all right. Give Darcie exactly what she wanted.

I approached the living room where the lighting was set and ready for a live interview as if Barbara Walters was in the house. The chairs face one another. I sit in front of the mystery woman ready for battle.

"Do you have anything besides a picture of my father, a birth certificate perhaps?"

"The father is listed as Unknown."

"Of course. So you basically have no proof."

"Only my mother's word. She has no reason to tell me something untrue."

"You watch the show, Distinguished Gentleman?"

"Yes. I watch it all the time. But I knew who you were long before seeing the show."

"Why did it take you so long to contact me?" Those nights watching legal dramas were paying off. I felt like a detective in the perfect scenario for getting to the truth.

"Like I told your producer, my mother encouraged me to seek out what family I had left. I knew you'd assume I was here because of seeing you on TV, but I wanted to honor my mother's wish. At least try." She closed her eyes and turned away. Conveniently facing the camera. "Maybe this wasn't such a good idea."

I saw a glimmer of familiarity in her profile. She had my nose but not my eyes, an overall likeness in the packaging. The tilt of her head, the boldness of her expressions, were mine. I simply didn't want it to be true.

I've met people many times who could be my sister, even brother, resemblance so strong you'd swear we were related. I believed the more logical point is that there's no determination of who's related to who. Generations where slavery bred brothers and sisters who were split up before ever knowing each other, meant you could be living right next door to someone directly in your bloodline. We could all be related by the barest of lineage.

Her DNA meant very little to me. What I cared about was the man I'd idolized my whole life, for it to still be true that he was the father and husband I'd looked up to. To care about one meant I had to be defeated by the other.

I searched past the blast of stage lighting for Darcie. "Are we done now?"

"I can answer that." Bliss took off the mic and laid it in the chair. She offered a polite smile to no one in particular before heading to the door. She stopped and faced me. "I don't know why I thought you'd be happy to see me. It was silly to fly all the way here." Her slim frame made her seem fragile and in need of someone to take care of her.

"Okay, wait a minute. I'm sure you can understand my skepticism. I'm not trying to be rude, but it's kind of dangerous to trust just anyone these days. Where are you staying? Which hotel? After I speak to my father, I'll call you." The camera was still filming. Required drama be damned. I didn't want to look like the bad guy.

Bliss quickly saw an opening. "I only came to meet you. After I saw the show, I figured you were so nice. I hadn't really made plans beyond that."

Nice? I'd been called many things, but that wasn't one of them. I struggled for a moment not sure what to do. I didn't want to throw her into the street whether she was telling the truth or not. Either way, she seemed harmless.

"The production company can put her up in hotel," Darcie interrupted from somewhere behind me. "At least for a couple of nights...until you two can work this out. Maybe things will be clear after you talk to your father."

Bliss reached out and touched my arm. "I'm sorry for showing up here unannounced. I'm just going to go."

"No. It's okay. I will make room for you." I wondered what's come over me. I touched my lips as if a ventriloquist had taken over.

"This is great," Bliss said as she wrapped her arms around me. "I'm so happy. I didn't know what to expect, but this is beyond my expectations."

I hugged her back. She smelled like peaches or something too sweet for me to stomach. I backed away. The minute I did, the doubt already crept into my mind. What had I started? You have no idea who this woman is and you invite her to stay in your home, near your children.

The house was so large, maybe I wouldn't see her. The Georgia style estate was excessively large. There'd been no middle ground when we were shopping for real estate. You either went big or went home. The house was a perfect fit for starting over, big enough to get lost in. What was one more stranger thrown in the mix?

Surely it wouldn't kill us.

Jump In, The Water's Warm

Bliss had only one suitcase. She unzipped it and pulled out her telephone. "Hey there. It's all good. I can't believe everything is working out just like you said it would."

She listened intently to the voice on the other end of the line. Listening had always been her strong suit. Memorizing was also a natural skill. She only had to see something once and she could recount every detail. She'd taken in the softness of the couch, the sheen of the glass table with pictures of their family. Jake and Venus holding each baby, side by side after they were born. The smiles on their faces told of the joy those babies brought to their life, but also the heartache they still felt for the child they'd lost.

"I will call you again when I can. Just know everything is going perfectly. My new family has welcomed me with open arms."

Bliss hung up the phone and put it back in the secret compartment of her suitcase. She hated being secretive and dishonest. Her grandmother would say, a means to an end can never do harm.

Her means was big, huge, and very real. She had one goal and until she reached it, she had to stay silent. No one would believe her if she told the truth. Especially not Venus. Her new sister was the epitome of believing only what she could see. Bliss bet she needed proof for every detail of her life. She probably made lists for every decision in her life, pros, and cons, to justify her every step and movement. Should I or shouldn't I? It was laughable watching her indecisiveness. Should I trust this woman, or shouldn't I? Any minute she was expecting the knock at the door. There to announce she'd made a mistake. What was she thinking?

Bliss shoved the items she'd been holding back into her suitcase. They would serve their purpose soon enough. Right on time. There she was knocking at the door. "Coming," she called out.

"Hey, um, I was thinking maybe you could chill out up here until I talk to...my husband about you visiting."

"No problem. I understand."

"I can bring you something to eat, a sandwich, something to drink."

"Actually, I have my granola. I'm not too big on processed foods. The nitrates make me itch," Bliss mimicked itching around her neck. "I'll stay in the rest of the evening. We'll talk in the morning."

"See you then."

Bliss closed the door. She wanted to dislike her, but found it difficult. She mostly felt sorry for her. She had everything, yet she was empty inside.

The phone began to ring. She'd forgotten to put it on vibrate. Besides, there was nothing more to report. As she'd said earlier, it was easier than she thought to make her way inside, now all she had to do was follow through.

Room Service

I slammed the book closed and tossed it on my nightstand. I pulled the chain on the lamp beside me and scooted down into the covers letting the pillows swallow my face.

I heard Jake come into the room. He was late getting home from a party thrown for one of his artists. I listened in the dark as he tossed his shirt and pants over the edge of the settee. He climbed into bed. His hand slid up my thigh and was headed west.

"Don't even think about it," I said in my best Dirty Harry voice. "Not here."

"Babe, even if there was a camera hidden somewhere it wouldn't show anything. It's pitch dark in here."

"Two words, night vision. All those reality shows where they think they're getting down and dirty in the privacy of their own beds and all you see are blue skin and white teeth. Not going to happen to me."

"Then let's go to a hotel."

"Maybe tomorrow when I can plan better." I squeezed my thighs together suppressing my own desire to make love to him.

"Yeah, nothing like a planned sex night to get the juices flowing." He rolled over and beat the pillow to submission.

"I'm sorry. Just not a good time. I was hoping you came home early so you could meet Bliss."

"Who's Bliss?"

"That's her name. The lady, remember, my sister, or maybe sister." I turned over and faced him. "Jake, I'm thinking we should pull back for a minute. You know all this attention from the reality show is bound to make all the freaks come out. If one more person knocks on my door and says they're related to me, I will run away from home. I'm serious. Maybe we could just tell them we don't want to do it anymore. I mean, we don't need the money anymore. You've got a steady stream of deals coming in."

"Yeah, but those deals are stemming from the Distinguished Gentleman. You know that, right? One's not separate from the other."

"Well maybe we could scale back. We have enough to float for a while now, right?"

"Scale back? As in downsize? We couldn't sell this house if we wanted to. There is no scaling back. Besides, you wanted to do this show too. As I remember, you were pretty excited about the whole idea."

I was silent remembering the exact conversation, or conversations as it turned out. We talked about it, researched, and ignored the fact that nine out of ten couples ended up divorced after doing a reality show. Soon as the camera stopped rolling and the lights went out, so did their love for one another.

We were better than that, I'd convinced myself. No matter how many times I tried to tell myself Jake and I didn't fall in that category, the facts spoke otherwise. We were fighting more, and kissing less. We'd planned for one season. Now we were filming season two by popular demand. Money was the main factor. The contract for the second season was double the price, but not the fun.

"Baby, you're right. It was my decision too. I just want you all to myself," I said, deciding to take a new approach. "And once we get these cameras out of here, we can go back to doing the things we like doing."

"I have an idea, why don't we go to a hotel, tonight. The kids are already sleeping. I checked on the twins before I came in our room. It's perfect. No one will even know we're gone." His smooth palm slipped under my arm and cupped my breast. My nipples instantly perked up betraying my stance.

"Honey, no. It's way too late."

"Fine, I'm booking a room for tomorrow," he said. "So get it together."

"Romantic," I answered back. "Will you buy me dinner first?"

"Nope. We have to scale back remember. You want romance, bring candles."

I buried my face in the pillow to silence my growl. I didn't want him to know he'd gotten the last shot in.

Papa Was A Rolling Stone

I knew this news would devastate my mother whether my dad was falsely accused or not. So I dialed my dad's rarely used cell phone. It was an old flip phone that he kept plugged into the charger outlet in his Toyota truck. Emergencies only. Like running to the store and forgetting what Pauletta told him to buy in the first place.

"Hello," he answered surprisingly on the first try. The three-hour time difference was a plus. While I was winding down from a traumatic day, his was just getting started. Though retired, he found a reason to leave the house every morning.

"Hi daddy."

"Hey precious. This is a surprise. Is something wrong?"

"Well, yeah. Something's happened."

A nervous chuckle. "Okay, now you're scaring me."

"Dad, do you know a woman named Millicent from about thirty years ago? Someone you may have been very close to." There was an edge to my voice, accusatory. I tried to soften things up a bit. "I guess thirty years is a long time ago. I just wanted to check with you because this woman came to my house—"

"Who came to your house?" Henry Johnston sounded suddenly grounded and serious. As a sales man for most of his lifetime, it was a habit and a skill to always remain affable. At home with Timothy and I, he stayed in his role as salesman and arbitrator, always looking for a solution. It would take a lot to turn him serious. Now was one of those times.

"Her name is Bliss. She claims you knew her mother." I was sitting in my car in the garage holding my phone with a warm tight grip. "I would've been about seven when she was...when you would've known her mother. Millicent. Is it true, dad?" I paused choking up. I decided to use Jake's line. "We all make mistakes."

"Bliss?" my father repeated.

"Yes. It's possible she's lying. Jake and I are getting pretty popular with this show coming on every week. Three million viewers. Pretty impressive huh. Bound to draw out a few weirdoes." I was already making excuses for my father.

"Yeah, I bet," he responded but still hadn't addressed any of what I'd asked.

"Millicent Gray, dad. Does her name ring a bell?" I sat holding my breath, still hanging on to the hope that it was the wrong Henry Johnston.

"Yes. I knew Milly a long time ago. Your mother found out and I ended it."

"Dad." I'm devastated by his confession. "And a daughter? Was that ever in the conversation while you were ending it?" His silence was too much to bear. "Answer me."

"Maybe it's best we have this conversation another time. I need to think about a few things."

"There's nothing to think about. You either knew about Bliss or you didn't. And if you did, how could you keep her from Timothy and me. We had a right to know. And mom...oh my God. This is going to kill mom."

"Your mother knew," he quietly admitted. "She knew about Milly and Bliss a long time ago."

****

It only took a few minutes before my mother called, infuriated by my father's report. "I can't believe you're letting this strange woman in your life. You don't know if she is who she says she is."

"How in the world could you keep something like this from me? You and Dad, how could you?"

"It wasn't my place. I wasn't the one who screwed another woman and got her pregnant."

"Thanks, Mom. I really needed that visual."

"Well, babies don't make themselves. I think we pretty much can agree on that."

"What other secrets do you guys have, huh? Maybe you have an additional child you forgot to mention?" I shuddered at the thought.

"So you believe her?"

"Why not? How many people know I have a sister floating around in the world? Of course I believe her."

"Well this is a slap in the face. I can't believe you're going to let her in your life, just like that. You have no respect for me."

"I'm sorry you feel that way. I just can't see putting her out in the street. I really think she has nowhere else to go. Her mother died. She didn't have any other family." I hoped it would evoke some kind of compassion.

"Can't you see she's using you? Whoever this person is, saw how well you and Jake were doing on TV and thought she'd snake her way into your world."

I held the phone away from my face. I couldn't listen anymore. My mother cornered the market on persistence. She would not let go of her point until I succumbed. "Okay, mom," I said to give in without truly waving the white flag.

"Don't okay, me. You better get rid of her fast and keep her away from my grandbabies. I know what I'm talking about."

****

Do you know who your parents are? Or *what they* are for that matter. The weight of their hypocrisy felt too heavy to bear.

"You're taking this pretty hard, huh, babe?" Jake sat beside me and put a comforting arm over my shoulder. He gave me a healing kiss on my forehead and it lingered ever so gently. "It's going to be okay. Everything's going to be okay." He'd been compassionate and patient letting me boo-hoo all day about my father's infidelity. He touched the corner of my eyes with the tissue he'd been holding.

"They're both liars," I sniffed into his shoulder too sad to be concerned about the camera pointed in my direction.

No rehearsal was needed this time. Sadness came natural. To think I'd almost forgotten what it felt like. I'd been too busy for wallowing. Taking care of the children. Sacrificing, compromising, arm wrestling with decisions all for the good of my family. But this news put a dagger straight through my heart.

Children spend the first half of their lives afraid to disappoint their mother and father. All this time I'd been lying about graduating from college with a 3.8 GPA when in truth I was barely getting by with a 2.5, or the fact that I was fired from my job in Washington DC, instead of my pitiful excuse of needing to stretch my horizons. I could've been my pitiful-self and proudly loving every minute of it instead of feeling guilty like I was letting my parents down at every turn. Who knew it was all just a Ponzi scheme to get you invested. Yet, there was no return.

Darcie clapped her hands as if it were the performance she'd been looking for. "Looks like we're ready for the next scene." We were already sitting at the kitchen table. She signaled and in walked Bliss looking expectant and surprised to see one big happy family waiting for her entrance.

Jake stood and kissed her on the cheek. "Welcome to the family."

She hugged him back with a firm clasp of her hands. She held on so long, Jake had to give her a firm pat as a signal to let go. Next she moved to me offering a mother of Theresa smile to go with her tear filled eyes. "Thank you. You have no idea what your acceptance means to me."

"I truly am sorry for the way I questioned you." I wanted to add that I'm also ashamed for the way my father had ignored her all of her life, pretended that she didn't exist. This was what made me sad. I made myself focus on the positive side. I had a sister.

She was taller than me. Her long silky black hair was worn in two braids with a bandana tied around her forehead. Her look fit with her nose ring. She must've wanted to make a good first impression earlier with her conservative bun and freshly pressed blouse and skirt. I can only wonder what her mother looked like. Millicent, or Milly as my father called her, must've been quite beautiful to lure my father. Or maybe she simply laughed at his jokes, or listened when he had something to say.

I tried to stifle these thoughts. Jealous of a woman I'd never met. I focused on Bliss. If you were going to have a little sister it was nice to have one that smelled like peaches, inhaling one more time before releasing my embrace. Her scent doesn't make me ill this time.

"Have a seat. I thought we'd have a big dinner so you could meet our children and friends. You don't have to go back to..." I forgot that quickly where it was she was from.

She smiled. "I was born in LA but I've lived in so many places."

"Lived? Well, where do you live now?"

She turned her head away easily telling that she didn't have an answer.

"It's okay. You know. You can stay here with us for a couple of weeks. I'd love to get to know you."

"You really are such a sweet person. And Jake, you're the brother I never had."

"Aw shucks. And you really are...well you're real. You're here." I hugged her and did my best not to say more than I should. I knew my mother was eventually going to see this little reunion at some point and I didn't want to gush over my father's biggest mistake, as if I approved of his ill begotten behavior. But it's not Bliss's fault and it's not mine. I think about our brother Timothy whose in Sudan with the Peace Corps, and can't wait to tell him the good news. A new little sister, birthed at 130 pounds, adorable to boot, delivered by the stork straight to my door.

Do Unto Others

How much money was left, that's all Sirena wanted to know. She owed a lot of people. One in particular who wasn't going to take no for an answer.

She sat across from her financial adviser, the fool who'd gotten her into this mess in the first place. Her eyes traveled over his head to the host of plaques and frames on the wall. Jarod Hayes, CPA with a host of other initials behind his name. She should've known better. Anybody who needed to tout every degree and diploma he'd earned since grade school was surely inferior.

She listened impatiently a few more seconds before bursting out. "Just answer the damn question."

"With your stock investments, you've got a net worth of $30,000. That doesn't include the fees and taxes for selling the shares." He clicked and tapped on his keyboard. "Minus another ten percent."

"What do you mean, another ten percent? Please tell me you're not trying to charge me for a commission after you've lost almost every cent I had."

"That's a little unfair. I didn't lose your money, the stock market dipped considerably. You're not the only one hit by this downturn. But my fee can definitely be waived until the climate changes." He went back to his keyboard and screen. The blue light reflected on his glasses. Sirena felt like knocking them off his face and telling him the climate change would be when hell froze over because she wasn't giving him another red cent.

"When the stock was dipping you should've jumped ship instead of letting me drown."

"I'm an adviser. I consult with my clients before I make drastic moves. As you might recall, you didn't respond to a single one of my six or seven messages."

"Just cash me out so I can get out of here." Sirena felt the pang of nervousness in her stomach. The doom and destruction of her life seemed never ending. Her career was in the toilet. What little money she had left she had to have in hand, not sitting around waiting for somebody to put a lien on it. The wheels were in motion. Too late to go back now.

"If I were you, I'd focus on parlaying this money into an investment. If you cash out, you're just going to fritter it away."

"Fritter...isn't that a pastry? I don't eat carbs. And furthermore, you're so fired, so you can keep your advice to yourself."

Days like this made her a danger to society. She was angry beyond measure. She backed out of the parking space and headed home. At least her home for now. The phone rang in her car. She answered without checking the caller ID by pressing the button on the steering wheel. Such a handy feature on her car. She loved her car but it would eventually have to go back to the dealer. She couldn't afford the $700 dollars a month lease.

"Talk to me," Sirena answered, not knowing who she was making the request to.

"Good afternoon, with who am I speaking?" The happy voice sailed past her speakers.

"Who did you call?"

"I'm calling from The Fireman's Fund. We hope you will help us support our local firefighters and their families this year."

"Oh please, they need to help support me." She pressed the button and hung up without a second thought.

When the phone rang again interrupting the music, she answered again, ready to tell little miss fire pants to take her off the call list. Instead she got a new caller.

"Hello, may I speak to Sirena Lassiter," the monotone voice asked?

"Ah, you have the wrong number." Sirena hung up. The bill collectors were circling. She could hear the piercing sound of her credit score dropping like a torpedo bomb. It was time to stop waiting for things to happen to her and start making things happen. She dialed the only number she knew that could save her.

His voice was music to her ears. "Hey there, CiCi, how ya doing?"

"Jay, it's so good to hear your voice. I didn't think you were going to answer. I've tried to call so many times."

"Yeah, well, been busy with the fam. You know we've got twins over here. A boy and a girl."

How could she forget? Sirena could hear the joy in his voice and it only made her want to pull over and be sick."Of course. I congratulated you remember? And those pictures of them on those magazine sites were adorable. How's Christopher doing? I miss him. I'd like to see him."

"Christopher is very happy. He's good."

"Can I see him?" She repeated her question.

"That's up to Chris. I've never stopped you from seeing him, CiCi."

"I know, but he doesn't pick up on his cell phone. Like father, like son, huh?" She stalled her next question for fear she already knew the answer. "Have you thought about me? Us?"

"CiCi, really, let's not go there. If you want to see Chris, lets work something out. Other than that, we have nothing to talk about."

"I think we have plenty to talk about. I would think if he had to make a choice, he would choose me. He's known me longer than you. What, you've been his father all of a year? I really don't think we'd want to make him choose."

"Just stop. We're not having this discussion. Like I said, if you want to see him, we'll work it out."

"Yeah, whatever." Sirena hung up. She wasn't too proud to beg. Although, she would've definitely put her demands on the table: the boy or a million in small bills. She really didn't know what she wanted. All she knew for sure was Christopher was her only link. Her only true path to Jay, and her only real block to that path came from his wife, Venus. Other than that, there was nothing else to know.

****

She'd cashed the check from the accountant. She wasn't comfortable gambling away what little money she had left. But like anything, no risk, no gain. She had to put it all on one number to get the big payout. She was more determined than ever to go through with it. Why leave anything to chance?

The man walking toward Sirena nodded. The sun directly behind him cast a shadow blotting out his face. She nodded cordially just in case. She wouldn't know what he looked like anyway.

The first time they met she was in a dark movie theater and he sat behind her and told her not to turn around. A bit dramatic like an old spy movie, but she obliged. This time she promised herself she would get a good look at him. She was about to hand over her life savings, what was left of it. The least she could do was know who he was.

"Nice day," the voice came from behind her. She attempted to face him before he barked his order, "Don't turn around."

"Oh please. This is ridiculous." Sirena twisted her neck around and was greeted with an open newspaper.

The man stood behind it. "I said not to turn around. I guess you have a few trust issues."

"Ya think?"

"Makes sense, you not being the type to wait around for things to take their course. You want it your way. Gotta be in control."

"What woman doesn't want to be in control? And if she says she doesn't, she's lying."

He chuckled. "So noted." The voice was strong but not dangerous. She guessed he was in his early forties. He was average build wearing jeans with a blazer. Very business casual with a near close-cropped haircut lined perfectly straight at his neckline. She took in as many details as possible.

"So what did she do to you? This woman, what did she do that was so terrible that you wanted her out of the picture?"

She was convinced there was no other way to break the spell that Venus had over Jay but that was none of his business. "So, what, is this therapy?" She turned to give him the side eye. His back was to her, still pretending to read the paper. If he recognized her as the famed Sirena Lassiter, he didn't let on. He addressed her by her phony name. "No one will ever connect you with the deed. You'll be spotless, Ms Sanborne."

She still had no information as to how it was supposed to happen, when, who, what, where. All she knew was that she would be the happiest girl in the world when Venus Johnston Parson, daughter of Pauletta and Henry Johnston, born on May 1st, 1970 in Los Angeles, California and married to Jake Parson on March 8th, 2004, was officially black history. She wanted her gone, destroyed and forgotten. Anything less than making her disappear would not be good enough.

"I just want to know when."

"I've already got everything in motion. That's what you're paying me for, so you can never know anything." He paused and rattled the paper enough to let Sirena know it was folded. "Can I ask you something?"

"No, you may not." She stood up, leaving all the money she had in the world in an envelope under the newspaper he'd eventually slipped beside her. She knew exactly what he wanted to know. Why did she need to go through all this? It was obviously over a man. She was beautiful, she could have any one she wanted. What was so special about this particular man that she'd kill for?

She adjusted her cap and sunglasses before taking off in a light jog. Her answer was simple. A beautiful woman needed a beautiful life, otherwise, what was the point.

As Luck Would Have It

Little pieces of memory were starting to come back to me. Like the day Pauletta threw all of Henry's clothing out the bedroom window. He didn't bother going outside to get them. It was Timothy and me who picked them up like it was a game. "I gotta shirt. I gotta tie. I got a sweater. *Eeew* I got dad's tighty-whitey underwear."

We lugged the clothes back upstairs and dropped them on the bed where neither my mother or father could be found. They were quiet fighters. Unlike my friend's parents where I'd heard too much, my parents never fought out loud. If there was ever yelling going on it was aimed at me or Timothy. Not each other.

"You have one choice. No options," Pauletta said coming out of the bathroom where they must've had their quiet discussions no one else could hear. "Did I ask you to pick up those clothes?" Timothy and I stood frozen. "Take'em back where you found them."

We gathered up as much as we could carry. We dropped them back on the lawn in the backyard. Although not nearly as scattered. I did my best. Timothy took my hand and pulled me back inside the house. "I don't think it matters," he said.

From the screened porch, I saw one last tie sail downward. She must've forgot one. No game. To betray Pauletta was like teasing a hungry tiger. I wondered what other punishment my father endured. What else had I missed?

I thought about the times I'd been angry with Jake, especially during the time he let Sirena get between us. I never really attempted to punish him, only make him understand how much he'd hurt me. Then there were the times I felt like the luckiest girl in the world. I trusted him.

It took a long winding road to get there. To trust anyone for that matter.

"There you are?" Jake sat down next to me on the rocking bench set underneath the covered patio. I didn't know how long I'd just been sitting, reliving past moments.

"Sorry, were you looking for me?" I pointed out toward the jungle gym. "Mya wanted to come out and play. Christopher didn't want to, so I told her I'd keep her company."

"You're such a great mother."

Those words nearly brought tears to my eyes. "Thank you, I was kind of worried about that. Feeling like I wasn't spending enough time with her, you, Christopher. Just feeling a bit thinned out."

He slid a hand between my thighs. "I can say unequivocally that you are doing a fantastic job."

"All right, mister, what's your angle? Is this about the hotel room?" I finally asked. "Cause, boy, oh boy, you're pouring it on pretty thick." I rolled my eyes, already knowing what was coming next.

"I'm a growing boy, I need to eat."

"Well, guess what, there's plenty of food in the kitchen."

"I don't want that kind of food," he whined. "And no, I didn't bother booking the room because I knew you would find an excuse not to go."

"Oh my gosh, I'm out here thinking about the meaning of life, and you're trying to feel me up." I plopped his hand back on his own lap.

He sighed with defeat and adjusted himself. He had serious wedge in his pants. I felt bad for making him wait so long.

He put his hand on mine. "I don't know where I'd be if I didn't have you in my life."

I cut my eyes in his direction. "Are you still trying to schmooze?"

"No. We're supposed to be thinking about the meaning of life. So, that's my meaning of life. You, my family, I'd be lost without you. Hopelessly lost," he said gently in my ear.

Men were either hungry or horny. If those two needs were met, life was usually pretty calm and satisfying.

"Let me go in and fix you a sandwich," I offered, hoping to buy myself some time.

"Hey there, you two." Bliss came out holding a plate of cheese and crackers. In the center was a beige unknown dip. "Thought you could use a snack. You're going to love it." She set it down between us.

"Thank you. That's so sweet." I was loving Bliss more everyday. "Wow, this is great, and just in time. Jake here was starving."

3 1613 00451 8810

CALUMET CITY PUBLIC LIBRARY

He smirked at me. I was first to attack the unknown substance. Only after I got a cracker full did I ask. "What is this? It's delicious."

"Oh, a combination of oysters, capers, Kalamata olives, chickpeas and a special blend of herbs. I call it the Ultimate Aphrodisiac." Bliss smiled and winked as if she'd listened to our entire conversation.

"I don't do capers," Jake announced. "Too tart for my taste."

"You have to try it."

"I'll just have some crackers," he said politely.

"He's very particular about what he puts in his stomach. If it's not certified organic and worth every calorie, not going to happen. He just finished a photo shoot for *Men's Fitness and Sports* magazine. The editor told him she'd never seen a body like his where they didn't have to use any airbrushing."

"I promise, I cook very light and I always use organic ingredients."

"Is that what you do...I mean are you a chef?" I still hadn't gotten any details of her life.

"I worked in a few restaurants, but I wouldn't say I was a chef. I think that word is very loosely thrown around. Let's just say I know my way around great ingredients and a perfect kitchen such as yours."

"Well, I don't have any photo shoots or editors to impress." I bit into the creamy dip. "Oh, delicious." I spread another.

"Enjoy. I'm going to go finish dinner." Bliss gave a baby wave before slipping her hands into her frayed denim pockets.

We've been sisters for exactly three days and I feel like I've known her my whole life. My mother called every single day to check on me, and give more warnings. "She's the devil's spawn. Anyone who would seduce another woman's husband, then flaunt the baby in your face is truly evil." Then I respond with, "Who the mother is does not dictate who the child becomes."

"Mommy, come push me," Mya called out.

Jake stood up. "I'll go. You look like you could use a nap."

I can't help but agree. I was fine a second ago, then I was suddenly tired. My eyelids felt like they had weights on them.

Jake helped me to my feet. "Go, babe. It's cool. Get some rest while the twins are sleeping."

New and Improved

At the kitchen table, I could hardly keep my eyes from blurring, no matter how much I blinked. I felt a step behind. Jake explained to me that I'd slept right into the night from my nap. He had to wake me up in the morning. I'm convinced the exhaustion of the show's tapings, arguing with my mother, along with my super mommy duties had finally caught up to me.

Darcie entered the kitchen. "Good morning, my favorite family. What'd we miss?" A rhetorical question since the first thing she did upon arriving was review the sound discs from the evening before. Then she started the day with a meeting to go over the direction, or in reality world speak, do-overs.

Christopher was by my side, too loud in my ear. "I said I'm going to be late, are you taking me to school?"

I tried to answer but nothing came out of my mouth.

Bliss breezed in surrounding the area with the scent of peaches. "I'll drive you." She attempted to direct Christopher away from me. He shook loose from her grasp. Bliss was so helpful. She looked like the picture of health. Her dark wide eyes are filled with excitement to start the day, the week, her whole life, it seemed.

I touched my head where the bubble of strangeness resided and all I can think was, when did I lose that twinkle in my eyes. I don't feel well.

"You don't know where my school is." He put a thumb and forefinger under my chin like he'd seen Jake do. "Mom," he let out an exasperated whine, "You have to take me to school."

The boy had no patience for stepping out of sync. He craved order from the first day he lived with us.

"Chris, relax, man. I'll drive you." Jake appeared wearing a lean T-shirt showing off his physique and a pair of dark jeans. "Babe, go back and lay down. You're probably catching the flu or something. You don't look good."

"You really should go lay down." Shelly's voice sounded distorted in slow motion. So many voices.

"Mommy, you don't feel good?" Mya kissed me on the cheek. "I'll take care of you." She put a soft small hand over my forehead to feel for a temperature. She had one more week of summer vacation and then she'd return to the Whitherspoon Academy. I was going to miss her light voice frolicking around the house during the day.

"There you are?" Gema approached holding Lauren. "We're ready for our morning feeding." Her thick Russian accent was the only one that sounded normal.

I touched my breast, remembering my job, the one that was truly important. To my shock there was no swelling, no firmness. No milk! "Wait. I need a minute." I stand up but have no idea what to do. "Wait, can everyone please just be quiet for a minute."

No one heard me. Jake continued to negotiate with Christopher. Mya was making a wish list for her day. Darcie and her crew were setting up for their shots.

I moved to the stairs one slow step at a time, wishing I could go faster. Why won't my feet move?

"Are you all right?" Bliss took me by the arm. "Let me help you. Maybe you should see your doctor. I can call for you, if you want."

"No. I'm fine. Just got off to a wobbly start. Do me a favor, keep Mya company for a while."

"Hey, where you going? We're ready to film breakfast," Darcie called after me.

Finally inside my bedroom I closed the door and found my phone.

I lay on the bed and watched as the room spun while I waited for the line to pick up.

"Dr. James office, hold please."

"No. Wait." I closed my eyes and hoped that the spinning passed.

The receptionist came back on the line. "This is doctor—"

"This is Venus Parson. I'm having an emergency."

"Then you should call 911. What's going on?"

"I don't have any milk," I blubbered. The room spinning seemed secondary.

The receptionist tone changed immediately. "Oh. Of course, let me get Dr. James on the line."

Dr. James came on the line. His comforting tone was always pleasant. An older man who'd seen just about everything in his lifetime. "How are you, Venus?"

"Not too good. I'm having trouble. I can't nurse the twins. I'm not ready to wean them. I don't know what happened. It's not time." My hand fell over my face. The spinning stopped.

"Okay, what I want you to do is go take a nice relaxing warm bath. The key here is relaxing. Lock the door. Put on some headphones. Sometimes too much stress will block your let-down process."

"Yes. Right. Okay." It made complete sense. I was under stress. An understatement if there ever was one. But what was I supposed to do? Tell everyone to get the hell out of my house. Maybe I could at least ask them to delay filming the reality series for a couple of weeks. Just the thought of asking Jake made my head pound. He needed this for his career. For all of us.

"See how it works out, then I want you to make an appointment for a full check-up."

****

I'd learned early in life, there was the beginning, the middle, but the end was all that mattered. No one remembered the awkward girl from high school when she showed up a bombshell at the 10 year reunion. The pain of the journey was only remembered by the one who'd endured it. From the outside, little else counted.

No one was sitting around the table worried about my lapse of energy, or recounting the details of my demise. All that mattered was that I was fine. Lauren and Henry had been fed and satisfied. The house was quiet as I peeped from room-to-room. "Anyone here?"

The kitchen looked like a commercial spread for a perfect family home in a magazine. Sunshine bounced off the spotless counter top so bright I had to squint. The place was clean and spotless with a new arrangement of flowers on the center of the gleaming tabletop. Vince made sure they were delivered twice a week. Since taking over *In Bloom*, he always made sure they were sent with a nice note. I flipped it open. "Missing you, Vince and Trevelle."

I finally heard voices. I moved toward the large window over the sink. Bliss and Mya were having a picnic on the manicured lawn. The red and white plaid tablecloth was laid out with Mya's play tea set. They sat cross-legged facing each other. Darcie was not far off with her headset and clipboard while the cameraman zoomed in to catch a lower angle of the happy pair.

It'd been a long time since I had teatime with Mya. Okay, at least a couple of years. Between running the floral business and having the twins, our quality time had been rare. Seeing that big smile on Mya's face made me smile too. Still, I couldn't help but feel a twinge of jealousy. She and Bliss toasting their plastic tea cups and taking sips before Darcie calls out, "Okay. We got it."

"We don't have to go in, do we?" Mya asked.

"Absolutely not. We can stay here as long as you like. In fact, I'd like a spot more tea, please." Bliss poured real tea from the bright pink container.

"Look, a butterfly." Mya gushed. Darcie flagged her hand, signaling for the camera to begin rolling.

The butterfly landed on Mya's open palm. A moment that precious had to be captured. I was also glad to share in it. I stood transfixed at the beauty of the two of them.

Bliss lifted her arm and another yellow butterfly landed. Then miraculously, two more just as beautiful.

"It's raining butterflies." Mya covered her mouth in astonishment.

"You know what this means," Bliss announced. "It means good luck. Make a wish. Go on, close your eyes and make a wish." Then there were several more butterflies. Too many to count.

I leaned closer to the window as if I could hear Mya's quiet whisper. Everyone knows wishes are never to be said out loud or they won't come true. But I wanted to know. What does my daughter wish for while her eyes are pulled tightly shut, while her lips move in long indiscernible sentences?

It must've been big. The kind of wish that only a child's lightness of heart could conceive. What would she know about needing a good night's sleep, or needing to lose thirty pounds, or desperately needing to know you're not ruining your child's childhood with each passing day.

Gold light seemed to be coming from everywhere. I looked up and around to see if the crew was using some kind of special effects. The sparkling dust surrounded Mya's head too. What I was seeing rooted me in the spot where I stood.

As majestic as the shimmering light appeared, it frightened me. I closed my eyes hoping when I opened them it would all be gone replaced with simple blue skies and a regular day in the neighborhood.

Please, I begged of my brain, make it go away. I opened my eyes and to my relief the glow over Mya's head was gone. *Thank you.*

"This is the best tea party ever," Mya announced, throwing her arms around Bliss.

We fear what we don't understand. I remembered reading that statement in a college coarse and it stuck with me. Since then I do my best to make sense of a situation and try not to judge what I don't understand. I said try, because right then and there I was ready to pack up the children and flee the house, convinced there was something out of my control going on.

I rubbed the chill off my arms and tried to replay the images, this time with a logical point of view. Like Dr. James said, stress affects everything. Throw in a little exhaustion from sleep deprivation and the world could be turned upside down.

"There you are?"

"Yes, here I am."

Bliss stood in front of me holding the tea party tray. "Do you want to join us?"

It seemed only seconds ago I was staring at Bliss through the window. I looked out to see if there was two of her. I blew out a long breath of relief when I saw Mya sitting on the blanket alone. "I think I'm going to head back upstairs. Can't seem to get my bearings."

"I can imagine. You've taken on a huge chunk of responsibility. All of these children. This house. A superstar husband. It's no wonder you don't just climb into bed and sleep for a week."

"I wish. But duty calls. I appreciate you spending time with Mya."

"Are you kidding? She's a joy. I'd love to have a daughter to spend time with. Children are so innocent and reassuring." She put the tray down and went to the sink to fill up the teakettle with water. "I met your mother once, when I was small. I remember that day like it was yesterday. I bet she didn't tell you that, did she?"

"There's a lot of things my mother hasn't told me."

"She came to our house, alone. She sat on our couch and offered me a piece of gum. My mother wouldn't let me have it. Guess she thought it was laced with arsenic or something. She and my mom exchanged a lot of mean things to each other before that day so she didn't trust her, her gum." Even with her back turned, I knew she was hurt thinking about that day.

"Bliss, whatever happened between our parents is in the past. I think me and you deserve our own fresh start."

"I agree."

"I would've loved to have had a baby sis back then. It makes me angry too, the thought of being kept away. Let's start our own future. Let them stay in the past."

"Thank you." She faced me with tears brimming. Fairy dust be damned. She was my sister.

Miracle On Venus Street

Having children makes you ask, what will they believe in, how will they cope with heartache? Who will they turn to when life gets hard? They needed to know someone was listening and that they weren't alone, or crazy. Such was the case as to how I was feeling after witnessing the dancing butterflies and gold haze over Bliss and Mya's head. No matter how I tried to shoo it away as my imagination, I knew something wasn't quite right.

Normally, we had Sundays free of cameras and microphones hanging over our heads, but Darcie's eyes popped with excitement when I brought up church. The thought of priceless moments filming in a black southern congregation ranked right up there with infiltrating a secret society.

Jake's manager suggested Tabernacle Baptist Church as our safest bet. The place met certain protocol such as large bouncer types at every entrance. The large salaciously built house of worship was made of stone and lots of glass. Most importantly, the reverend couldn't be linked to any sex scandals, at least so far.

The choir sang. The preacher preached. I prayed.

I took a peak over at Darcie. Her eyes closed and her head bowed, she was probably asking for ratings. But who am I to judge. My prayers included a laundry list of demands. All of which required money. Comfort. Joy. Peace of mind. To think at one time I believed happiness was free.

After the service, we waded through the crowd who wasn't fazed by the film crew. Out to the sun filled lobby enclosed by glass walls three stories high, patrons of faith and amazing handbags gathered for hugs and how-you-doings. I saw Keisha moving in our direction. Her stride across the lobby was smooth as if the place wasn't filled with people at every turn. If anyone dared cross her path her six-inch high Louboutins would trample them leaving smashed toes in her wake. Keisha was tall and model lean. Her megawatt smile opened as she approached. She was a pro and didn't look straight into the camera hanging over my shoulder.

"Good morning, Parsons." Keisha leaned down and gave Christopher a kiss on the cheek. "Hey handsome." He melted into simmering boy goo with the compliment. "Jake, I just spoke with Gordon Dempsey. He has a script he wants me to take a look at with you in mind." Church and networking seemed to be synonymous. She faced the rest of us. "Did you enjoy the service? And you must be Bliss. I'm Keisha, Jake's manager."

Bliss was distracted, taken in by each celebrity she saw. Atlanta had become the weigh station for black celebrities, actors, musicians, and reality stars. We were just part of the crowd. But Bliss saw things differently. She squealed with delight when Raj Madera came toward Keisha and planted a kiss on her lips. He was an all star basketball player who wanted to turn his next career into movies.

"Oh my goodness, this is just too much." Bliss fanned her hand in front of her face. "I remember when he played on the Bulls."

"You lived in Chicago?"

"I've lived in a lot of places," she answered defensively.

"Oh." I left it at that. I wasn't the FBI. Not like I needed to trace her whereabouts for the last thirty years. I figured I'd get to know her over the time she stayed with us, but information was difficult to get out of Bliss.

Admittedly, the week had flown by and we hadn't got a chance to share like I'd hoped. Seemed I was always tired so I was spending more time in bed, determined to keep my milk production steady.

The celebrities kept coming. "Is that...?" Keisha patiently nodded every time Bliss pointed to a familiar face.

"There are a lot of celebrities that go to this church. They come here because they know no one is going to make a big deal about it." She hoped Bliss got the hint and didn't run up to anyone, which would get her tackled by the cleverly spaced bodyguards.

"This is so exciting. You guys are surrounded by a lot of famous people."

"Don't over react. They're only human just like us," Keisha said.

"I guess," Bliss said, looking around the church. She was wearing a dress that used to be mine. I couldn't fit ninety percent of what was in my closet. On Bliss it fit like a glove on her gentle curves. I found myself imagining again how beautiful her mother must've been.

I peered over at Jake and wondered if that was all it took to lead a man down the path of least resistance. Beauty. He was surrounded by beautiful women quite often and today was no different.

Church ladies used to be big hats, paper fans, and pantyhose. Not to mention minty fresh breath with kind words of praise. These days the definition had changed sharply. The women wore tightly fitted dresses with open cleavage, bare legs in high heels, and that minty warm breath was eager and ready to spread hot secrets and promises they probably couldn't deliver.

I knew the look in their eyes all too well. When I saw one of the women stroke little Henry's curly head then let her hand conveniently fall to Jake's arm, I wanted to scream, "don't touch my baby," or my husband. However, I'm no longer allowed unreasonable outbursts. By noon my rant would've entered the Internet's gossip stream and become the noise of an unstable, unhappy, jealous wife and I am none of those things. Not anymore.

"Look at that, just shameless. That one may as well be arrested for public lewdness." Bliss whispered near my ear. "Don't worry, those women have nothing on you."

"I deal with that kind of thing all the time. No big deal," I said partly annoyed she'd caught me staring in Jake's direction. I took a deep breath. Lately it seemed I could never get enough air. Always wondering if the air had been turned on.

"You're a stronger woman than me, that's all I have to say. I couldn't take all that attention doted on my husband. And why doesn't he just tell them to respect his space?" Bliss squeezed her jaws tight and narrowed her eyes.

"They're harmless. And he certainly can't go around being rude to admirers. He wouldn't get very far in his business."

Jake cradled Henry's head before kissing him on the cheek. One of the church ladies plants a kiss on Henry too.

"Did you see that?" Bliss whispered. "Who has that kind of nerve to be kissing on someone else's baby when they don't even know you. You have a right to go over there and snatch him."

"Snatch who? Jake or Henry?" I rolled my eyes. Bliss didn't understand. It was part of the life. You were either in or you were out. I touched her elbow. She was entirely too worked up. "Trust me, it's okay. Time to go," I said loud enough with a cordial smile, but she didn't seem to hear me.

The touchy feely woman whipped out her phone and gave it to someone to take a picture while she snuggled up to Jake. She had one hand holding Henry's head against her bosom as if she'd given birth to him and the other stationed around the proud papa's waist. I turned away feeling that strange sensation in my stomach. Angst. Apprehension. Exhaustion. All rolled into a tight ball that I continually had to swallow but ignore the pain.

Suddenly a woman shrieked. I turned to the ruckus and saw the woman next to Jake pulling at her dress.

"That' ought a teach her," Bliss snickered.

I rushed over to see what was going on since the crowd quickly blocked my view. I wanted to make sure Henry and Jake were okay. When I pushed my way through the crowd, I saw the woman who'd been grabbing on Jake. She was screaming at the top of her lungs. Her entire dress was torn open, her cheetah print bra and matching panties on full display. No matter how she tried to cover herself, the buttons wouldn't close. Either her dress seemed to be shrinking or she was growing. One of the other women handed her a couple of church fans to cover her expanding front view.

The security guards were on the case and took the woman by both her arms. They weren't listening to her pleas of innocence. This kind of public nuisance would not be tolerated.

"Always a party at Tabernacle Baptist, huh?" Keisha poked her head between us. "I'm going to get going. I'm meeting my mother for brunch. You know, she'd love to see you all if you want to join us."

I was too busy trying to digest everything I'd just seen to answer Keisha's invitation. "You saw that, right? Her dress?"

"I think everyone saw it," she said. "The camera got it all. Who knew your husband had that effect on women? Got the poor woman stripping in church." She grinned before putting her cheek against mine. "Never a dull moment around you guys. Kiss, kiss." She moved her other cheek against Jake's. "I'll call you in the morning. I've got some good things to discuss with you." She was off.

I was stuck, unable to move, the same way I felt looking out the window at the pixie dust circling Mya and Bliss earlier in the week. But this time, Darcie directed the cameraman to stay on the woman until she was no longer in sight.

On the ride home, I was dying to ask Jake what happened, his take on the whole incident. But I had other things I wanted to say too that couldn't be mentioned around Bliss. Instead, we rode in silence all the way home. Darcie and her crew followed not too far behind in a large white van. Jake maneuvered to the security gate and waited patiently while the gate opened slowly as possible.

"My gosh, good thing nobody's got an emergency. This thing needs a tune-up or something."

Jake reached out and touched my hand. "You all right? You've been worked up since we left church. I thought it was supposed to make you feel better, all of us going as a family, not make you more anxious." He eased his foot of the brake.

Up the winding driveway then waiting forever for the garage to rise. I tried to relax. I was ready to burst. I wanted to talk about what I saw. I knew what Jake would say.

I was making assumptions, that's what he would say. The same as when I'd accused Darcie of planting the porn DVD under Christopher's mattress so I would conveniently find it while being filmed. She insisted that I confront him about it on camera. How very convenient. I wouldn't do it. And I destroyed the DVD. Why would Darcie do something so awful? He'd asked. I answered, because she'd do anything to make her job easier. She was like a cop who needed to close her case and go home. If she got enough film in the can, her job would be complete.

I had no proof of what she did, but I knew my gut instinct wasn't wrong. Jake wanted to ask Christopher about the DVD but I made him swear not to say a word. I knew the worst thing you could do to a child was show distrust, especially if he wasn't guilty. But this wasn't the same. This was bigger than gut instinct. I'd seen the strange happening with my own eyes.

Jake put the car in park. Christopher was already unfastened from his seatbelt and climbing out the back of SUV. "Dad don't forget you said you'd play another battle game of Galaxy Sky 10 with me."

"Yep. Glad you're ready to take your beating like a man."

"Yeah right." Christopher laughed.

"Can we have another tea party?"

I turned around to oblige only to see that Mya had been asking Bliss, not me.

"Can we keep on our dresses and wear some hats so it's like a garden real tea party?"

"Absolutely," my new magical sister answered. She saw me turn back around. "Venus, you'll join us, won't you?"

"No, you guys go ahead." I hoped she couldn't read minds. She'd know I was onto her.

Mya leaned over the center seat and kissed me. "You'll feel better soon, mommy. Then we'll have all the tea parties we want." Bliss and Mya climbed out next. The back of it seemed to go on forever, but with a family of six, there weren't many options.

Gema arrived and unsnapped the baby's seats. Henry clapped and bounced when he saw her. "*Hellzo*, my angels. Did you miss me?" She transported them one at a time to their indoor stroller. She was what I called a genius of invention. Pretty creative when it came to moving the twins from point A to point B. She rolled off, pushing the babies effortlessly into the house.

I took off my sunglasses after everyone was out of the car. I turned to Jake and grabbed his arm before he made his exit. "I have to tell you something. Promise me you won't say I'm crazy."

"I listen to everything you say." He touched my chin. "What's going on?"

"Okay. I think there's something strange about Bliss. I mean, not bad strange, just different strange. She's got some kind of power to make things happen."

"We all have that power, babe. Some people just never tap into it." He nuzzled my neck.

"I'm not talking about *The Secret*, think your thoughts into action kind of stuff. I'm talking about making something happen like black magic, or Voodoo."

"Why does she have to be a witch, or a voodoo queen?"

"Did you see that woman's dress pop open just like that? How else do you explain it? What if she's some kind of—"

"Fairy, or a leprechaun?"

"Stop it. You said you'd listen. I'm serious here. Call it whatever you want. But I've seen it. I was watching her and Mya out the window and there was this gold sparkling light surrounding them. Then this flock of butterflies landed on her arm."

He nodded as if he was waiting for the big finale. "That's it?"

"Jake. I'm telling you, there's something weird going on. And the lady today, after she was flirting with you, suddenly her dress unsnaps like a ghost was working those buttons."

He leaned toward me. "Maybe she ate too much dairy and the gas blew up her stomach."

I pushed his face away so he could see I was serious. "I knew you were going to say it was nonsense. Maybe you're right. I've been kind of off kilter. My head is constantly spinning."

"Babe, it was a coincidence. Nothing more. Maybe she was dressed so brightly the butterflies thought Bliss was a flower. And maybe the ladies' buttons were loose. You want magic, I'll show you magic." His fingers trailed the buttons on my top. It easily came undone since I usually wore tops that had easy access for nursing. "Well look at that, your dress popped open."

"We can't."

"I bet I know what will make you feel better." He kissed me lightly on the lips then pulled me in for a full frontal. His kisses certainly were magical, I could attest to that, the power to silence me and make me forget everything going on. My head swooned with a dizzy mix of lust and desire.

"Its time, babe. Six weeks has long passed," he said, letting me know he'd been counting. "I promise you'll feel better. All your tension and stress will be gone." He kissed me again and danced his tongue around the fullness my bottom lip.

"Six weeks is for one baby, I had two. So technically, it should be twelve weeks."

"Twelve weeks are long gone." He took my hand and placed it on his rock hard dilemma. "Long gone."

A make-out session in the car was hardly my idea of a good time. But in all honesty it probably was the only safe quiet place, which was half the reason I didn't want to do it in the house. I was afraid our love making would end up on digital feed, visually or in sound bites.

His warm mouth gently moved to the tip of my breast. The tingling sensation followed with instant swelling from his touch. His tongue swirled and tugged causing a surge of pressure. Next time I have trouble filling with milk I knew exactly where I'd go.

"You're going to get me all wet."

"That's the goal."

"I mean, my breast. You might get more than you bargained for."

"Even better. I missed you, baby. I need you." There wasn't much more he needed to say after that. His sexy voice in my ear sparked heat I hadn't felt in a long time. My body ached for him to be inside of me. I sank underneath him as he pushed the seat all the way to recline. Making out like teenagers included feeling like it was our first time. So many months of touching and kissing but not going all the way. My tangled panties fell to the car floor. I moaned and grunted to my hearts desire. I didn't care who might hear. The height of satisfaction sent me sailing high overhead to a place I'd almost forgotten but would never forget again.

Jake and Venus sitting in a tree, K-I-S-S-I-N-G.

****

We stumbled in with guilty faces. Jake more so than I. "Don't make me wait that long again." He gave my bottom a firm squeeze. He'd been such a bad boy clearly written all over his face. The grin evaporated when he saw the woman standing over Christopher, both her hands resting on his shoulders.

"Hi," she said, as if it was an everyday occurrence that she should be standing in our kitchen.

"Why are you here?" Jake asked before I could.

"I told you I wanted to see Christopher. Remember, you said it was up to him. Well, only way I was going to find out was to ask. So here I am."

I faced Jake with a questioning glare. He responded with a small shake of his head, in other words, not here, not now.

"Why are you in my house?" I said before I could stop myself.

"I guess I'm here to see my son. You have a problem with that, we can always discuss a new agreement," Sirena said turning her eyes to Jake as if he knew exactly what she was saying. "Is that what you want?" She asked daringly.

"What I want is for you to get out of my house."

"Venus, obviously what you want has never really mattered."

"Hi. I'm Bliss."

I'd almost forgotten we had an audience. Bliss extended a hand to Sirena. I was tempted to warn her to take her hand back before she got bit. Snakes were quick. But on second thought, they may have been equally matched. I wondered if Bliss could make Sirena disappear. Now that's what sisters were for.

"And you are, the new nanny? And so cute," She did a tisk-tisk and gave me a knowing roll of her eyes.

"She's my sister," I said with pride.

"Wow, I see the resemblance. Kind of a taller, better looking version" she said to me without looking in my direction. "Nice to meet you. I'm Sirena, Christopher's mother. His real mother."

"Mya, are you ready for the tea party?" Bliss saw where the reunion was headed. She quickly took Mya's hand and led her out the back door.

"Alright, that's enough," Jake intervened. "Outside," he said to Sirena.

"I will not leave. I'm here to see my son." She emphasized the 'my son' part, but there was no heart in her words. She had one agenda, pure and simple.

I was ready to defend myself, but I could see the intensity in his dark eyes. "Babe, let me talk to Sirena for a minute," he said leaning in my direction and pulling me close. "I'll be right up. Let me just handle this real quick."

"Okay," I said, but felt my blood pressure shooting to the moon. I focused on Christopher and didn't want him to see me act a fool. "Okay. See you upstairs. Christopher, you want to go upstairs. I'll play Galaxy 10 with you."

"Why would he want to go upstairs when I'm here to see him?" Sirena asked. She put her hands on her tight dress hips.

Jake put out his hand to direct me out.

Her eyes glared at the moist spots on the fabric of my dress. She cleared her throat like she was suppressing a laugh. "Nice seeing you."

I went quietly leaving Jake to handle the situation. I vowed to never do the dirty fighting ever again when it came to Sirena Lassiter. She was out of my league and I knew it. Her fangs were longer. Her claws were pointier. Her tongue was sharper. I was no match.

It took me a minute to leave entirely. I listened. Not because I don't trust Jake. I simply didn't trust Sirena. She would never leave us alone. We would be old and gray and she'd still pop up, ready for a come back, a retry for Jake's attention. I wondered if she liked the drama or if she really believed she stood a chance. There's no telling with someone like her.

Jake started first. "You can't come over here anytime you like. Why don't we make arrangements for tomorrow? I'll bring Christopher to meet you."

"I kept asking and you kept putting me off. I just needed to see my son. Our son."

Right.

"Not cool, okay. Even worse is for you to come in here and disrespect my wife. I'm only going to say this once, don't come here. If you want to see him, we'll meet you."

"Why is this suddenly about her?"

"You made it about her the minute you came through that door knowing it would piss her off."

"Actually, she was the furthest thing from my mind. Like I said, I'm here to see my son. You miss me, don't you Christopher."

There was only silence. I hated that he had to sit in the middle and be involved in her manipulation. But what other bargaining chip did she have?

"Things are going horribly wrong for me and I need to be around the people who love me."

"I'm sorry to hear that, but that's no excuse."

"You don't care anything about me. You won't even talk to me."

"I've asked you to respect my house, my wife, our agreement."

"Fine. Tomorrow then. How about lunch? We'll meet at Bison's."

"I will be in school tomorrow," Christopher announced in his voice of reason reminding everyone this was supposed to be about him. "Then I have piano practice. After that, I have math tutoring."

"Fine, it'll be dinner then."

"Cool. Can we go to Red Robin?"

"What's a red robin?"

"I don't want to go to that other place. They only serve raw meat, and raw meat isn't healthy," Christopher protested.

Bison's, the upscale steakhouse was where celebrities went to be seen. She'd taken him there in her previous life when she'd been pretending Christopher was her baby brother. Even when the tabloids were labeling her the best liar, she showed up for photo ops with a big pink smile on her lips determined to have everyone believe she did nothing wrong. It was way too late to start a PR campaign for mother of the year now.

"Fine, six o'clock."

"Oh, yeah, I forgot about baseball practice."

"You? You play a sport?"

"He plays a lot of things," Jake said finally ready to end the charade. She had no idea what Christopher did with his time or hobbies, favorite foods, allergies, all the things a mom should know.

"Whatever. You can miss one day," Sirena snapped. "I'm not waiting all night for you to play in dirt."

"Jake, can we please go to Red Robin? They have shakes and fries. That's where I want to go."

Sirena interrupted. "You'll eat wherever I say you're going to eat. It's my hard earned money. When you can take care of yourself, we'll eat where you want to eat."

Christopher's voice took an older more serious tone. "You don't take care of me, Jake does."

"Hey, buddy, why don't you join Mya and Bliss outside." Jake seemed to have had enough.

And so had I. I didn't want to hear anymore.

"They're having a tea party. That's for stupid girls."

"Watch your mouth," Jake chastised. "Either outside, or upstairs."

"Fine. I'm going to my room."

I heard Christopher coming and moved the rest of the way up the stairs before he saw me. I needed to find Gema anyway and give her a good scolding about letting just anyone into the house. I could see the dilemma. We were running a circus. All the attention-starved species were circling the feeding wagon.

I entered the nursery but the lights were out. Gema had already given the twins their bath and put them to bed. She slept in the room next door with the baby monitor on. It still hadn't worked in giving me more sleeping time. I could officially label myself an insomniac. I listened for their every sound, their every hiccup or cry. I leaned over Henry's crib to stroke his cheek and he gurgled a happy reply. He was wide awake.

"Hey, little guy, you were waiting for mama to say goodnight?" I scooped him up and held him close. I warmed my face against his smooth cheek, inhaling his sweet baby scent. "Mommy's here." No sense putting him back down in the crib if he was going to be wide awake like his mommy. I took him with me.

After a while I heard Jake coming down the hall. Our bedroom door opened slowly with caution as if he expected me to hurl something his way.

"Don't worry, you're safe," I said bouncing Henry in my lap. "Who's that, huh? Is that daddy?"

Jake's face lit up. "There's my little man."

Henry reached out, anticipating stronger arms. Jake gladly picked him up, giving me the opportunity to pick up the book I'd been reading when I had quiet time, How to Speed Up Your Metabolism. Losing weight while nursing for two wasn't recommended. However, I was feeling horrible lately, sluggish, and losing steam before 12 in the afternoon.

"Boy, you're getting big. Look at you." He turned his attention to me. "I'm sorry, babe. I swear I had no idea she was going to just show up like that." He sat on the edge of the bed. Henry now reached back for me. There went my reading time.

"You and I both knew she was going to show up eventually. As if she really wants to spend quality time with Christopher. She doesn't even like the boy. I can hear it in her voice. She's just trying to get to you."

"I told her I'd take Christopher to meet her for dinner tomorrow. That's all."

"I don't trust her. I really wish you wouldn't leave him alone with her."

"Fine, I won't leave him."

"Okay," I said to Henry, "Guess mommy really fell into that one."

Henry bounced showing his smiling gums. He pushed himself forward for a wet one. His big brown eyes were swallowed up behind his chubby smile. I gave him a smooch.

"What about me, don't I get a kiss?"

"Nope. No kisses for you."

"I knew you were going to blame me for this."

"I don't...I know it's not your fault. You can't control Sirena. No one can."

"Yeah, she doesn't take rejection well. I have to handle her my way."

"I swear, I was this close," I paused, realizing Henry didn't like the tone of the conversation. His little lip pouted and was about to go into quiver mode. I had to pull out the big gun and give Henry exactly what would put him at ease and to sleep. A full stomach. I let him nurse while Jake looked on with admiration.

"I know how to deal with Sirena, okay. Trust me."

"Oh, I do. I trust you. She's the one I wouldn't turn my back on."

"Looks like he's sleep." Jake stroked a hand over Henry's head. "Want me to take him to his crib?"

"Sure. But put him on his stomach in case he releases air. But not flat, you know, make sure his head is turned."

"Babe, come on. I got it." Jake lifted him with ease.

I opened my book back up and tried to pretend I wasn't worried about everything under the sun. Besides, I already had too much on my plate to be consumed with what Sirena was up to. The fact that I couldn't recall exactly what was on my plate didn't bother me the slightest. All I knew was my world was filled with the business of parenting and managing a household. Nothing left for Sirena. Nothing. She didn't deserve any of my time or attention.

Made You Look

The moon peeked through the enormous trees surrounding their palatial estate. It really got on Sirena's nerves to think Jay and his brood could afford such a big house when she couldn't keep hers. She returned home from the fiasco of a video shoot in Miami to the eviction notice posted on her front door for the entire world to see. At least she'd been paid cash. Not bad for sitting around looking pretty. But it wasn't enough. Even if she caught up the payments on the mortgage, there'd be nothing left and she'd land right back where she started.

Sirena looked up after every few feet as she backed out of Jay's entrance. She couldn't ignore the feeling as if someone was watching her. The place was lit up like a Gingerbread house. Yellow light cast from every window and arch. Only thing missing was a roof made of frosting.

She wished the entire place would catch on fire, but then she couldn't wish that or she might lose Jay in the process. She took back the wish. No, what she really wanted was for Venus to disappear like a cloud of smoke. Only her.

The nerve, she fumed. *Just gon walk out of the room like I'm not her biggest threat,* she thought growing more aggravated by the second.

She checked the rearview mirror as she backed out but kept her eyes on the house too.

Like I don't matter.

She couldn't stop the surge of anger. She had good reason to be angry. "Just let me handle this real quick," she hissed in a low voice. Like she was trash he needed to take out. "Yeah, you handle me."

There was an overall contempt for the Johnston Parson household. Jay for being so gullible, Christopher for being so easily swayed to the other side, and all that damned unity. Freakin Brady Bunch. She knew they were only faking it. Christopher was nobody's favorite child. He was a handful to say the least. Venus probably kicked herself everyday for letting that little pain in the ass stay with them. Fakers, all of them.

Who did that...who faked it anymore? This was a time to be real. Take the gloves off, smooth some Vaseline over the cheekbones and start swinging. Maybe that was it. Venus was no fighter. All the more to Sirena's advantage. She'd go down with one hit. "Oh yeah, your time is coming." She spoke her claim out loud. Speak it and so it shall be. "You're going to get yours, you can believe that."

She did her best to calm down. But, damn it she was mad. She was tired of just thinking and wishing and hoping. She was ready for Venus to be washed away as if she never existed.

She looked up one more time to see someone in the window looking out. *Yeah, that's what I thought.* A satisfied smile rose across her face. She looked again wanting to get one more chance to gloat having accomplished her goal of getting under wifey's skin. "That's right. I'm that bitch," she sang the words to one of her hit records. "You better recognize."

But on closer inspection she saw that it was someone else. This person had straight hair cascading over her shoulders. Venus wore cornrows like some regular chic. No added hair, just her natural mane in five or six giant rows across the scalp and landing on the low side of her ear, a clear sign she was out of her league. If she were Jay's wife, she'd give him the respect he was due and be fly every single day.

Sirena shook her head in disbelief before putting her focus back on where she was driving. Maybe it was the nanny. Or Bliss, the convenient new sister. She chuckled. So damn gullible.

She slowed the car to focus more closely but the figure in the window had already disappeared. She checked the other windows. So many. She guessed there were at least ten bedrooms. Obviously, Venus was on a quest to fill every one of them with children like some kind of mating cow.

Sirena couldn't have children for which she was grateful. She'd made sure of that the day Christopher was born. At nineteen, she was wise enough to know kids were more trouble than they were worth and would only interrupt her life. Besides, Jay would be all too through with the whole baby-in-tow thing by the time they united. Venus was running some kind of daycare center in there. Blinding colors of yellow and red plastic toys everywhere. When her time came with Jay, they would have great adventures, travel and have hot sex. And by chance if Jay wanted more children, she'd convince him to pick one up from Somalia or Louisiana like all the other power couples in Hollywood. A child was a child, what difference did it make where it came from.

She only hoped Venus didn't pop one more bun into the oven before her plan was put into effect. First his wife, then his unborn child. The scenario would destroy Jay. He'd be an emotional wreck and flat out, no fun. She didn't have time for coddling him while he healed. She wanted to get on with the business of living. They had hit songs to make and movies to star in. All she wanted was the magic. The two of them had created it once, they could do it again. He was the key to her life. But there was no way of convincing him of that with Venus around.

Her phone rang while she was driving. Though it was against the law to talk and drive at the same time, she couldn't ignore who was calling. "There's a complication that's going to require another ten grand," the man announced without hearing her say hello. This irked her to no end. What if she had been someone else?

"What exactly is the complication? You know what, maybe I need to find someone else."

"Tomorrow. At Dunne Park," he said unfazed by her threat.

She hung up and hoped he wasn't trying to shake her down for more money. She'd already given him thirty grand, which seemed a bit pricey. Not that she'd investigated the going rate for a hired killer. But really, it was a day's work at best. How complicated could it be. She wondered how often he got calls like the one she'd placed. Right out of the Internet yellow pages she let her finger do the scrolling. She randomly selected his company under private investigators. Red Target Investigations. A woman had answered on the first ring, took her name and number and said someone would call her right back.

Within the hour, he called. "How can I help you, Ms Sanborne?" Using the fake name she'd given him.

"I want information about someone. I want to know everything about her family, her life, ex's, siblings, everything. Anything you can find to prove this woman is no saint. She's too good to be true, and I want to make sure her husband knows."

"No problem," he'd said. "I'm kind of expensive, are you sure that's all you need?"

It was as if he'd read her mind. The silence on her end only confirmed what he suspected. "In that case, we'll need to meet in person."

Disappointment shrouded her mind. She regretted having to make these kinds of decisions. None of this was her fault. She didn't understand why she was being punished. She punched the gas harder even though she could barely see more than the hood of her car in the darkness. What if it didn't work? What if her plan crashed and burned?

She hit the steering wheel, still angry about what... everything, anything, she wasn't sure. She fanned herself then punched up the air conditioning. It was October, no reason to be this hot.

She veered slightly to the right when something jetted in front of her car. Before she knew it she was swerving again to avoid a ditch with pylons in the middle of the street. She slammed on the brakes and skidded to a stop. The engine shut off. She put the gear in park then tried to start it back up.

It gurgled and sputtered but didn't turn over. "Great. That's just great."

She pushed the emergency button on the overhead panel. She'd never used it before but knew it was supposed to send out an instant signal. Nothing happened. No voice chimed in like in the commercials to save her from falling into a ditch.

Then she remembered that was part of the satellite service that had been recently turned off. Another bill for something she didn't really need, until now of course.

She tried the engine again. All the panel lights came on but the engine only sputtered. She pulled out her cell phone and started trolling through the address file realizing she had no one who gave a damn about her. Once the checks stopped coming, her relatives and so called friends dwindled down to zero. Her cousin, Quincy, used to be her bodyguard but now worked as a bouncer at a strip club. Whenever she called him, he always pretended to be too busy to do her a favor. Especially since that favor didn't involve cash.

If she called a tow truck to come out in the middle of nowhere it would run her close to three hundred bucks, and since she didn't have any cash on her and her credit cards were past their limit, she was screwed.

She landed on Jay's name. He would come. He wouldn't say no to a damsel that needed rescuing, no matter how much Venus would protest and say it was all a manipulation to get him out of the house. He'd still come, that much Sirena knew. She touched Jay's name, the number dialed.

She waited for the phone to ring. The line hung empty filled with air but no Jay. She hung up and dialed again, this time using the voice system. "Dial Jay," she demanded.

Nothing. She sat in the car with only the light coming from the dashboard.

"Call Jaaaay," she enunciated. The phone responded as if it had a mind of it's own, 'sorry, there is no such number.'

It made no sense. Who would've deleted his number from her phone, or even had the opportunity. She'd had her purse under her arm the entire time at Jay's house. She didn't know how, but somehow she could blame Venus for this too. Somehow she'd figured out a way to lift Jay's number out of her phone. Maybe she'd hired a hacker. Or even, just maybe got Christopher to use his geeky genius skills against his own mother.

It was too hard to believe. She tried again. And again. Until she gave up and finally dialed the tow service.

While she waited for the tow truck, she reclined her seat and tried not to be afraid of the dark. But her skin began to chill with goose bumps when she heard a noise outside. Was it someone's laughter? She cautiously opened her eyes and looked around. There before her was the silhouette of someone with long flowing hair blowing in the non-existent wind. A girl. No, a woman, she decided. Older she guessed by the way the moonlight reflected the shimmering gray on her hair.

The woman was walking towards her, but more like floating. Sirena sat frozen. She tried to focus to see more clearly. Who-in-the-hell? She couldn't see her face. Sparks of light came out of nowhere giving her only a glimpse but Sirena could've sworn it was her own face she saw. Wrinkled and old. Tired and weak.

Sirena hadn't been afraid of anything in her life. Fear and weakness were not an option in her chosen field. She summoned the old Sirena, the one who'd defied the odds and got a recording deal with a major studio when she was only a teenager. No matter the obstacle, she was the girl who kicked the door down and fought her way to the top even though every step she took seemed to be met with a slippery slope. She'd almost forgotten all that she'd accomplished.

"Your ass is about to get ran over." She turned the ignition. Miracles of all miracles, the car started. She threw the car in drive. With her eyes closed she pressed on the gas full tilt. She hoped the lady knew to get the hell out of the way because she was coming through.

When she looked in her rearview mirror, the woman was still standing as if the car went straight through her.

She couldn't see her face, but she could tell she was laughing. Laughing at her.

Fairy Dust and Lemon Rind

Morning was the favorite time of day for Bliss. She awakened feeling regenerated and filled with hope. Her heart felt light and filled with gratitude. She noticed it was only after coming in contact with adults did her mood drop or change. Children had not yet been destroyed by the harsh realities of life. They had no agenda. Whatever his or her needs may be at the time, it had nothing to do with destroying anyone else in the process.

Bliss flipped the cover off and jumped out of bed. She wanted to get up early this morning to make Mya and Christopher breakfast. It was the most important meal of the day. Her grandmother taught her how to cook. Always fresh ingredients. Foods from the earth had the power to heal anything that ailed the human body. Equally so, were the ones that could harm the central nervous system, causing the body to shut down. Natural ingredients did not sit in the body like man made chemicals. They eventually flushed out without a trace.

She rushed a shower. Threw on a T-shirt and jeans. She tied a scarf to hold back her hair and then applied a light layer of blush and lip gloss. Thankfully the kitchen was all clear. The film crew took up so much room with their bulky equipment. Not to mention, having them looking over her shoulder at all times. She pulled the tiny envelope packet out of her pocket. She sprinkled a bit of the brown powder that could easily pass for cinnamon in a separate bowl and sat it off to the side. She couldn't have done that with the cameras watching. She pushed the packet back in her pocket and began to stir in the rest of the ingredients.

Before the noise of footsteps, she knew someone was coming. She looked up and saw Jake. "Oh, hey, can I get you some breakfast?"

Jake responded too quickly. "No. No thank you," he said moving past her. He seemed annoyed.

He couldn't have seen anything. Her back was to him when she opened the packet. Bliss would know if he'd seen something, simple as that. She turned back around to her bowls. She cracked the brown eggshell and let the contents fall keeping the yoke separate. If he wanted to be ignored, she would do just that.

Jake went to the refrigerator and reached inside. He shook the container of green liquid before opening it and taking a swig. A few seconds went by and he took another drink but said nothing. Perhaps he was tired of having too many people in his home.

Most men were easy to read. She could hear their thoughts coming from a mile away. Jake was different. Either he had very little on his mind, or he'd learned how to manage his energy. But she could guess what was really bothering him. He didn't like being in a woman's company unless she was part of the admiration society. Perhaps she should compliment him or make him feel special. She'd done none of that. She'd never heard his songs or seen his movies. Lying was something she wasn't good at but she'd try, just this once. "Can't wait to hear what you're working on these days. I'm a big fan."

"Thanks, enjoy your day," Jake replied, putting the now empty container in the sink.

"Yes, you too. We should find some time to connect."

"Yeah," Jake replied with about the same enthusiasm he'd shown earlier. Which was far more preferable than having him ogle her, the classic power move. Jake Parson wasn't like that. He'd probably never chased after a woman in his life. Why would he have too, a man like him? He was used to being chased. He was used to the attention. And because Bliss hadn't given him any, he didn't like her.

That was fine. She wasn't there for him.

Upstairs with the door closed, he'd probably warned his wife of the dangers of having a strange woman in their house. Someone they'd never met under the very same roof as their children.

She had to stifle a laugh from escaping. "Yes, be afraid, very afraid." She dropped a half cup of organic sugar in the pancake mix. One cup of milk. One cup of flour. She heated the skillet. Did her best with their commercial grade products. Obviously no one in the Johnston-Parson household took cooking seriously.

She said a short prayer over the hot skillet before pouring the first batch of pancake batter. "Bless this food, may it help the children grow strong with wisdom and pride." She took the other bowl and poured what was left of the batter, stirring slowly. This prayer was different. More of a chant inside her head. She repeated the last words out loud, *"Etena sacca vajjena sotti te hotu sabbada."*

Jack of All Trades

Jake was frazzled when he entered our bedroom. He put a finger to his lips as if he didn't quite know which words to use. "I saw something. What you said about Bliss is real, her being different like..." he trailed off in thought. "Something's just not right."

"I thought you didn't believe me. What's happened? What'd you see?" I stopped towel drying my hair to focus on him.

"I didn't say I didn't believe you. I said, why did she have to be into voodoo or black magic? Those kinds of terms are always associated with people of color. You should know how I feel about that." He sat down, still holding his thinking man pose.

"Okay, so...fine. Stereotypes. I was guilty," I said to move him along. As many times as he'd lectured me on how he hated stereotypes, I should've known not to use those terms. He'd been treated like some kind of thug during his music career as a hip hop artist, when in truth he had a college degree and had spent much of his youth classically trained on the piano. He hadn't shot or robbed anybody to make a buck. He was an artist, a musician, and a smart businessman. But in the real world if you quacked like a duck, you were usually a duck. If you cast spells and made ladies dresses pop open and threw fairy dust around it was hard not to call it as you saw it. I mean, I wasn't passing judgment or anything.

After he'd remained silent too long, I asked again. "Please tell me what's on your mind. What happened? Did you see something? Did she make like a spoon move across the table? Come on, I promise I won't tell you you're crazy like you did me. Oh, I got an idea, we can have her zap Sirena and turn her into a houseplant. That way she'll always be around, but silent."

Jake stood up and wrapped his hands above his head. Now I could tell he was seriously bothered to the point of pacing. He was a doer. He spent a finite amount of time hashing things over. He made an assessment of a situation and that was it.

"Honey, for God's sake, use your words. I was just kidding about the Sirena part. I don't think I would let her in our house even as a houseplant. Really. Tell me, what's wrong."

He took another deep breath. "I don't know. That's just it. I usually have this instinct about people."

Yeah, people that don't include Sirena. But instead replied, "Okay, go on."

"Well, Bliss...she's a locked vault. Her eyes are so cold."

"Okay. Everybody's not going to spill their guts. You haven't really spent any time with her."

"Wait a minute, first you're telling me she's got some kind of magical powers and that she's scared the mess out of you, and now that I tell you I sense something weird too, you're trying to plead her case."

"Honey, I don't understand where this is coming from. What did you see or sense?" I was starting to shiver from only wearing a towel. I pulled my robe from the edge of the bed and slipped it on.

"I can't put it into words. I think we should ask her to leave."

"No. I'm not going to ask her to leave. I mean, really? You're the one lecturing me about stereotypes and judging people, and just because you have this weird feeling you want me to ask her to leave." I shook my head. "No way."

"Listen to me, I'm not comfortable with her in this house."

"That's not enough," I repeated. "This is my house too, and I want her here."

He stroked his goatee a few times before making his next point. "You're right. I probably came off a little heavy handed. But what is your plan, exactly. You're just going to wait around for her to do something else that haunts you through the night. You can't sleep as it is."

"I can't sleep because I worry about the babies," I admitted. "I'm afraid. I'm always worried." I swallowed back the lump in my throat.

Jake came and kneeled in front of me. He took both my hands. "Babe, Henry and Lauren are fine. They're healthy. Nothing's going to happen to them. What happened before was just nature and God."

"I know. But what if nature and God rule against me again and..." I didn't like to talk about it. I hated that Jake even made me face this demon lurking around in my mind, fear.

"Nothing's going to happen to them, okay. You have to know that."

"I don't take anything for granted, that's all."

"So you rather sit up all night doing what, worrying never solves anything. You have to know and trust that they're going to be fine."

I let my head fall into my hands. "Agreed." I was glad he couldn't see my eyes or he'd know I was hardly in agreement. I knew nothing for sure except nothing was ever a given. There was no safe place. No way to hide from inevitability if the path was already set. Sometimes, you just had to be prepared for the worst, and then maybe even the smallest rise above it would feel like success.

He stuck his face in my hair and inhaling the conditioner I used before planting a kiss. "I love it this way. I wish you wore it like this more often, like you used to, all wild and sexy."

"It's a tangled mess. Now I have to wet it again. After hashing it out with you for the last hour I'll never get the comb through it."

"Then leave it like it is," he said.

"I can't. I think I was frightening the twins. Every time I went to pick them up, their eyes would pop open really big, like oh my gosh, it's the fro monster."

Jake started laughing and so did I. He seemed relaxed again. But he still had the thing with Bliss on his mind. "I love you," he stated matter of factly. "I'm just trying to keep you safe, okay."

"I know. I appreciate it. You know I listen to you, but I've enjoyed her being here, despite the weirdness going on. I've gotten closer to her, more than I have to anyone in a long time. I trust her, Jake. I do. I'm not going to just shove her out the door because she's a little different. Somehow, I think she's good for me."

He pressed his palm to the cool skin of my cheek. "I thought I was all you needed," he said semi-jokingly.

Because it had been true for a long time. I'd depended on Jake to fulfill my every need. Along the way I'd let my besties fall to the wayside. But there was no replacing the camaraderie of female friendship. I missed having a close girlfriend in my life who gave good secrets and made my nuttiness seem reasonable by scale. Since having the twins, I hadn't spent much time outside of the house besides the baby's check-ups and grocery store runs. Extreme motherhood had made me even more closed in and vulnerable. In the midst of life's storms, girlfriends were the anchors that kept you from floating out to sea. I craved the solidarity.

"Knock, knock." Bliss stood at the door holding a tray. "I brought you breakfast. I was hoping you'd still be in bed." She held the tray high on her shoulder. The smell of pancakes, honey smothered berries, and bacon float and swirl around my head.

"Come in. Look at all that food. Today was supposed to be the start of my diet." My stomach flipped and lurched me toward the tray. I shoved the crispy slice of bacon across my tongue. "Oh my goodness. Umm, this is delicious."

She set everything up like a five star restaurant on the round glass table in front of the fireplace. Jake and I had the bedroom laid out like a hotel suite but not once had we eaten on the table. "Honey, come on, this'll be fun." I hugged Bliss. "I can't believe you did all of this. Hot coffee. Whip Cream on the side. There's even freshly squeezed orange juice."

Jake stood near the door still waiting for her exit.

"Bon appetite," Bliss said before skipping out the room.

Good food was my weakness. "You see, hon, is this amazing or what? A meal this size is going to make me want to jump right back into bed and go to sleep for another couple of hours." I inhaled the goodness and convince myself it will be worth every bite. I put a fork full of pancake dripping with buttery syrup to my mouth. Out of nowhere, Jake took the fork out of my hand. He laid it back on the plate.

"You're right, a meal this size isn't really what you need right now."

I searched his face, speechless. He'd never commented on my weight. Not once. Not even the day we came home from the doctor's office after I'd tipped the scale at 240 pounds, he simply hugged me and smiled. "You've never been more beautiful," were his words when I cried in panic. I'd doubled myself.

I pulled the robe tighter across my chest, suddenly feeling exposed.

"What I meant," he said, witnessing the shock and hurt on my face, "is that I agree with you. Something this heavy is just going to slow you down. Why don't you try one of my green smoothies this morning." He shook the wrong words out of his mouth. "Babe, I'm just saying I don't think you should eat the food she gives you."

I picked up the fork and shoveled a double load into my mouth. "Umm, delicious," I said with a full mouth. I took another helping until my jaws were packed to the brim.

"Listen to me," he said suddenly hugging me. "I wasn't implying anything about your weight. I just spent the better part of the morning telling you I don't trust her and you're shoving her food into your mouth. If you're so worried about the twins, you should also be worried about what you eat, since it goes directly to them through your milk."

I pushed out what was left into a napkin. I knew he was concerned about the food, but I still thought a small percentage of what he said was talking about my weight. I elbowed him in his rib. "So what now, are we going to run lab tests on everything she cooks? Jake, really, I don't want you to feel this way about her. Today, I'm going to get to the bottom of it. I'm going to ask her point blank about everything."

"So you think she's just going to tell you, just like that?"

I hunched my shoulders. "I don't know, but I rather ask then wonder."

There was another knock at the door. I figured Darcie had arrived. Time to get to work. "Yes?" I sang out. Jake gave me a look. "I know, it works to make people think you're happy when you're not."

"Trust me, it's not working," he said. He went into the bathroom to get dressed. I went and opened the door.

"We have hungry tum-tums," Gema said, holding Henry and Lauren.

"I'll come to the nursery. I just need to throw some clothes on. I passed the mirror before going into the closet. I felt like an inflated balloon and looked like one too. It was time I took the weight serious.

Jake came out of the bathroom. "You're beautiful okay. Just stop it."

"No, you're right. I should give the smoothies a try. I'm going to get serious about getting this weight off. You're right," I said again. "But only about that part. I don't think Bliss would try to hurt me or any of us."

He gave up pleading his case. "Okay. Just be alert, okay." He kissed me goodbye and left the room with his car keys in hand.

"You're not going to wait for Darcie?"

"I've got an early meeting," he mumbled on his way out. "See you later."

I started toward the nursery where I knew Gema was doing her best to keep the twins distracted on empty stomachs. I filled up with the tears I'd been holding inside.

I stood outside the nursery and talked myself into getting it together. Hormones. Exhaustion. Being about fifty pounds overweight. All could ruin your day.

"Are you all right?"

The voice startled me.

I turned around to see Bliss. She opened her arms. "Oh, what's wrong? What happened? The food wasn't that terrible, was it?" She gave my back a soft rub. "You want to talk about it?"

"No. It's okay. I really am okay. Sometimes the hormones just get the best of me."

"I can only imagine. I bet you'd love a nice vacation with just you and Jake, huh?"

With those words, I started again. I couldn't hold back the sobs followed by more hugs from Bliss. "Oh, no. Did you two have a fight?"

I nodded and sniffed. "It's okay. We're okay. I'm just paranoid about gaining all this weight. You know, he's really into his fitness. It's not like I have a lot of free time to work out. So just the littlest thing can make me self-conscious."

"You're a nursing mother, you have to eat. Don't rush it. You'll be back in shape in no time. I can help. From now on, you and me are going to wake up and work out together. How about it? Gema is here in the morning with the twins. While Mya and Chris are in school, nothing stopping us, right?"

"Right."

"We'll start today."

"Okay," I agreed, though my body already felt sluggish and the day hadn't even got started. "I better go feed Lauren and Henry."

"Okay. When you're ready, I'll be ready." Bliss gave another hug. "What are sisters for, to make everything better."

One Step Closer

I blotted the sweat from my brow, feeling proud. The lethargy went away about a mile into the walk. Bliss hardly made a sound compared to my panting. A half an hour later, I needed to stop. I hunched over and rested both hands on my knees.

"You okay?" Bliss put her hand on my shoulder.

"I'm flat out done. To think I used to run five miles. Look at me."

"This was great for a first time out and you know what, I was doing my best to keep up with you."

I stood up, knowing she was only saying that to make me feel better. But telling a white lie for one thing usually meant it was easy to tell one for others. "Bliss I have to ask you something." I waited a few seconds to see her expression. She simply had a question mark. No fear of what I might ask. "Do you practice some kind of different religion, or umm, do you know how to create things that aren't there?"

She put her hand to her face and covered her laugh. "What? Why would you say that?"

"I know. I don't know. I'm sorry. It's just that, I've seen a couple of things with my own eyes, and—"

"Well who else's eyes would you have used?"

I must've looked horrified and she felt sorry for me. "I'm kidding," she said, giving my hand a gentle tap.

"Forget it."

"I'm just a little bit surprised by the question. I didn't know I was creeping you out. I guess you heard me chanting?"

"No. You chant?"

"I do. I can teach you some of it. It's a good way to cleanse your thoughts and get energy." Bliss opened her arms and spread them to the sky. "Here, out in nature is the perfect place. Come on, we can sit under the shade. I know the perfect chant for you."

I cleared my throat. "That's interesting but I have to get back, feed the babies, you know." The last thing I wanted to report back to Jake was that I'd chanted in the middle of the forest with Bliss.

My cell phone began to ring right on time. "You see, this is probably Gema. Wanting me to get back." I unzipped my pocket and pulled it out to see my father's name on the caller ID. I was glad it wasn't really Gema. A call from her wasn't good. But I also didn't want to talk to my dad in front of Bliss.

"Hey you," I answered instead of my traditional 'hi daddy'. After Bliss took a few steps away to stretch I whispered, "How are you, Dad? Everything okay?"

"Your mother is on her way, I thought I'd warn you," he said in a lower whisper. We were competing for who could sound more ominous.

"Coming here? Why?" I whispered back.

"She thinks you're in danger."

"If she's not there, why are you whispering, dad?"

"Oh, right." He cleared his voice. The phone can now breathe. "I took her to the airport and I just got back. There was no talking her out of it. She's got a full plan to be on your doorstep by dinner time."

"That's just great. Really." I rubbed my temples. As if I didn't have enough problems. The cloud cover pulling together to unleash a torrent of rain on my head was at the top of the list. Followed a close second of wishing I had a ride back to the house.

"She's got it in her head that the girl is out for some kind of revenge."

"What girl?" As if I didn't know. I rolled my head up to the sky. The one person who was on my side, who wanted to support me, and she was being attacked from all sides. "First of all, whatever do you mean? You think Bliss might be angry she was abandoned? Could that be it?" Sarcasm could not be avoided.

"I should've been there for her and her mother, I know that. But, you know how your mother is. I had to make a choice."

"I know, dad. Trust me, I know. But it's the past. You know what, you're the one who should be on your way out here. Maybe everyone would feel better if you just stepped up to the plate and said your sorries, to me, to mom, to Bliss." I try to calm down. "I really believe it's never too late to tell someone you love them. She might heal really quickly with one of your hugs. They always fixed me," I said, determined not get too emotional. The result would be the whizzing sound in my ears like a dentist drill. I'd been noticing that it came and went, but mostly came when I was angry, or upset. I planned to control my attitude all day.

"Aw, Precious."

"Please come," I said hoping the gentle approach yielded results. I needed a hug from my dad as much as Bliss probably did.

"Let me think about it, okay."

"Sure. Call me and I'll have a car waiting as soon as you land. Okay?"

"I'll call you," he said without commitment. Lately, I could see how good he was at that, avoiding his responsibility. The men in my life always were held in high regard unless they proved otherwise.

I was a card carrying member of the Benefit of the Doubt club. I never assumed the worst about a man and always hoped for the best. But if things went south, the gavel came down hard. I wanted swift justice. Only with my father, I didn't know exactly how to handle it. He was my dad, daddy. How was I going to support him on this, I just didn't know?

"I'll be here, dad. Okay. It's your decision, just know that I'm here for you," I offered, though my heart was wrenched with ambivalence. I hung up ready to go, get back on the trail and find my way home. Maybe I could fix this myself. When my mother arrived, I would sit her down and explain. No, demand that she accept Bliss for who she is, not who gave birth to her. Women had been healing themselves from the error of men's ways for centuries. Why should anything be different now? I was determined to fix this.

It took a minute to realize I was alone. I looked in every direction before I yelled, "Bliss, where are you?" There was a humming noise coming from a distance. I listened carefully until I realized it was her voice. She was chanting in a steady rhythm. What was she saying? I couldn't understand a single word. I followed the sound of her voice.

A full turn, then a second, and a third, checking in every direction before the dizziness hit. I could only describe what I saw as a summer white blanket cascading around my face. The nearly translucent and billowing sheath of energy wrapped and tangled around me until I couldn't catch my breath. I struggled to get air. Never had it crossed my mind that it could be me who left Henry and Lauren. I'd worried about them being taken from me but maybe it was the other way around. I saw it all in one sweeping moment. Jake dressed in black holding my babies while they cried in his arms. Mya and Christopher standing by his side as the dirt was tossed on my grave.

No. I couldn't do it. I refused to leave this earth before my children. I gasped for air, reaching for anything or anyone that could stop me from falling.

I didn't know how long I'd been on the ground. Before I knew it I was waking up. Bliss was staring in my eyes. Her hands were wrapped around my face. "Venus, are you okay? Can you hear me? You just blacked out. I caught you before you hit the ground. Do you think you can sit up?"

"My water," I managed to etch out of my dry mouth. "It's in my pack." She handed it to me. Water had never tasted so good. The small bottle was emptied within seconds. I'd forgotten to take even a sip while we were walking. Now, I had an unquenchable thirst.

"We should call 911," she said. "You shouldn't walk anywhere."

"No. I'm fine. Really. I'm okay." I looked her in the eye. "What were you saying out there? Bliss, tell me what's going on."

"Come on. Let's get you home."

"No. I want you to answer my question," I demanded weakly.

Bliss helped me to my feet. She still smelled like fresh peach cobbler. How ever did she do that? "What you heard was *Etena sacca vajjena sotti te hotu sabbada.*

It's a prayer. The simple translation is, may you forever be well. I've only practiced Buddhism for the last ten years."

I swallowed hard, feeling guilty. "I guess I've never known anyone who...I feel bad for asking you. It's none of my business. I didn't understand it."

"It's simple," Bliss said, "I prayed for you to be well, that's all."

"That's it," I asked.

"Yes." She smiled.

I believed her.

Mother Knows Best

Of all days, the security guard called from the entry gate to ask if it was okay to let a guest in by the name of Pauletta Johnston. I was tempted to say, "Who? That name doesn't ring a bell." Where was the courtesy call when Sirena had stormed the gates or Bliss for that matter? Though I was glad to have Bliss now, things could've turned out a lot differently.

"Sure, let her in." I checked myself in the mirror one last time. A little bit of sunshine and exercise did a body good. Even with my falling out episode on the walk, I looked rested. My mother would see me looking happy and healthy instead of the nervous wreck I'd been all morning.

The doorbell rang a few minutes later. I ran before Darcie or her minions had a chance to follow me with a camera. Surprisingly, there was no Darcie, no camera within hearing distance. Where had they gone?

"Mother, what a surprise," I said without the actual excitement. "I can't believe you came all this way just to see me."

"I came to see my grandbabies and make sure they're fine." She moved past me and looked around. "Go on outside and pay the taxi."

I already had my wallet in my hand. I tucked it behind me. I remembered I wasn't supposed to have information about her surprise attack. "Okay, Let me get my wallet." My mother stopped driving about five years ago when she was diagnosed with breast cancer, opting to wait for my dad to scoot her around.

I came back from paying the driver with my wallet a hundred bucks lighter. However I did gain an extremely large, heavy suitcase that I dragged into the house. Pauletta Johnston was nowhere to be found. I snapped to alertness remembering her true goal. She'd come to seek and destroy. I moved with zip speed up the stairs and landed directly in front of Bliss's bedroom. I listened as quietly as possible though my heavy breathing was hard to slow down.

Heaven only knew the possible damage Hurricane Pauletta could inflict, but to be honest, I was more afraid for my mother. Even after I'd tried to convince Jake that Bliss was harmless, I knew what kind of strangeness she was capable of. I'd seen enough. I didn't want my mother to be turned upside down or walk in to see her spinning like a bottle top.

Hearing nothing there, I moved to the other side of the hall to the twin's nursery. I heard my mother's voice cooing to the babies before I opened the door.

"There you are."

She held Lauren and Henry almost effortlessly, one in each arm. Tiny hands pulled at her lips and masked her eyes. They knew a grandmother when they saw one.

The nursery walls were painted like an enchanted rainforest. A large tree with a happy koala swung from a vine. A waterfall appeared to be gushing out of the right corner. Vibrant flowers peeked from green foliage. At every turn the room was a full fledge adventure.

"Henry's so big. What are you feeding him? And poor little Lauren just isn't getting any of the good stuff. Is big brother eating all the food? Huh? You can tell grandma."

I answered for Lauren. "Technically, he's my little brother. I was born first by six minutes." I looked around. "Where's Gema?"

"I told her to take a break. Grandma is here now. Yes she is, yes she is," she baby talked.

I saw Henry going for my mother's nose. I slipped in to take him off her hands. He's got a mean pinch. "Come here, big boy." He targeted my chin instead. I kissed his hand. "Be nice."

"Look at my grandbabies. I don't know why you all have to live so far away. It took me all day to get here. Five hours in the air, another two sitting around people who made me itch. You need to come on back to Los Angeles so I can spend time with my babies."

I took a seat on the tiny piano bench in front of the miniature keyboard. So far all the twins did was bang their hands on the keys. Jake already had their music teacher lined up to start lessons by the time they turned two.

"I'm glad you're here, mom. We miss you. Mya's going to be ecstatic. But you honestly didn't have to travel all this way. We're all doing fine. And you know, I would've picked you up from the airport. What's with the reconnaissance mission?"

"I had to see for myself," my mother answered without looking in my direction. "I know how you are. You want every one to think you got it so easy. I didn't want you staging happy just to make me comfortable."

"That's not true." I smoothed a hand across Henry's cheek. "I have everything I've always wanted. I have a family and a beautiful home and a husband who loves me. I couldn't ask for anything more. But the truth is, I get tired. And right now, I really don't need you coming here making me feel like I'm doing something wrong."

Pauletta gave me the look, the one that said, what-in-the-world are you talking about? She narrowed her eyes. "I'm not here to make you feel bad. I'm here to check on my grandbabies."

"That's what I mean. By needing to catch the first thing smoking to check on your grandbabies, you're saying I'm not trusted as a mother. And damn it, if nothing else I'm a good mother." I felt the tears welling up in the corners of my eyes. "Thank you for coming to check on us, but we're fine."

"So where is this new sister of yours?" she asked getting to the real point of her visit.

"Somewhere around here. Probably in her room." I kissed Henry on the forehead. He became excited, realizing he had me first for his noon feeding. I was food on wheels. Sometimes it was hard to accept that the babies may only see me for one purpose. I looked forward to the day when they knew I was the one they could count on. When they knew I would always have their back.

A lot like my mom, as hard as it was to admit. She always meant well, but her approach was a bit harsh.

"So has she done anything weird yet?"

"What do you mean?"

Pauletta flexed her eyebrows. "I'm guessing you know exactly what I mean."

At that moment there wasn't much else to do but confess. "I do. I know."

"You should've listened to me and sent her packing."

Money For Nothing

After the scare Sirena experienced, she'd hardly slept. She couldn't let it go. There was something entirely real about what she'd seen no matter how much she tried to write it off as her imagination. Sitting on the bench in the middle of Dunne Park, runners skirted by without so much as a glance in her direction. She must've looked as tired and pitiful as she felt since no one had slowed or did a double take. In the old days she couldn't have gone anywhere without being noticed.

She pulled her baseball cap lower over her full wavy tresses and adjusted her sunglasses. For once in her life, she was glad no one recognized her. She fingered the envelope in her purse that held the last of the jewelry she owned. Rings, bracelets, and a couple of necklaces. So much money wasted. Back then dropping ten grand on herself was just child's play. Nothing better to do would turn into a shopping spree so unreal, the credit card company would call and ask if it was she making the purchase or had the card been stolen. She always felt like saying, no. It wasn't her. But then they'd freeze the account and her day would be over. Not when she still had shopping to do.

Now it was worthless to her. The dull Korean guy at the pawnshop tried to give her a measly five thousand for everything. She answered silently with her middle finger and left. She was nearly to her car when she heard the whistle. The same guy was standing on the side of the building. He waved her over. She kept some distance between them while he stayed hidden on the side of the wall.

"What?"

"I know somebody who'll buy it. All of it, for a good price too."

"Okay. Where is this somebody?"

"Write this number down."

She pulled out a pen. She didn't trust her phone anymore. It had a mind of it's own. The ink rolled on her palm. She held up her hand. "Is that right?"

"Yeah, you call. Today."

She couldn't think of any other place to meet. Since it worked out with her mysterious assassin, a jewelry exchange would be a cakewalk.

The time was passing and it was getting late. She wanted to have a spa day to get ready for her dinner with Jay. Finally an older man who matched the voice on the phone walked directly up to her.

"Kwon's friend," he questioned with his extended belly too close to her face.

"Who? Oh yeah, sure."

"So what've you got?"

Sirena expected a bit more discretion. "Do you want to sit down?"

"Nah, I'm good standing."

"Okay." She pulled out the big padded envelope. "Same thing is in there that Kwon already saw. It's worth about $50,000. There's a six carat diamond in here."

"Not anymore. Gold is worth more than diamonds right about now, lady." He stuck his nose into the contents and actually sniffed it. "Okay. I'll give you six."

"Six what? Grand? Are you kidding?"

"Hey, you can do better in this economy, be my guest."

She wondered what happened to the old fashioned rule of fair play. Everyone wanted something for nothing. First the guy who wanted to be paid before he'd even done the job, one she probably should've had her cousin do for half the price, and it would've been finished already. And now this guy who was trying to rob her in broad daylight.

"Okay, whatever. Six grand."

He conveniently pulled out a white envelope then a separate piece of paper. "I need you to sign this and date it saying you sold me your property. I'm not going to be accused of stealing."

"Why not? That's exactly what you're doing. Stealing." She scribbled her name as illegibly as possible.

"Don't spend it all in one place."

"Fuck you," she snarled.

Sins Of The Mother

I'd heard the patent Pauletta speech from third grade on. *If only you would've listened to me. You're so hardheaded. Gotta do things your way. Well, look how things turned out.*

Though this time the speech was a bit longer.

"...never want to hear what anybody else has to say," she continued while pacing with Lauren in her arms. "I told you, didn't I? That girl's mama was the same way. You want to get all high and mighty and blame me and your father for not telling you the truth, when you would've never believed me anyway. Bad enough you didn't listen this time while my precious grandbabies are under the same roof as that girl." She stopped pacing as if something struck her memory. She turned statue still.

"Mom, are you all right?"

"It was a long trip," she said stealing another kiss from Lauren's smooth cheek. "Just worried about my babies."

"Bliss isn't my enemy, mom. She's not yours either. Children shouldn't carry the burden of their parents' mistakes."

My mother smirked at my naiveté.

I rolled my eyes and caught myself before she turned around. More of me not listening. When would I learn?

"I'm here for one reason, to make sure my grandbabies don't suffer for their parents' mistakes."

"You mean grandparents'," I added with a bit of scorn.

"Your father's mistake, not mine. I didn't sleep with the hussy and knock her up."

"How did they meet?"

"You should ask your father that question."

"I'm asking you."

She took a deep breath then carefully sat in the rocking chair across from me. Lauren and Henry were the happiest about this seating arrangement. They extended their bodies reaching out to each other.

"She was a waitress at a café he frequented. He claimed he didn't remember sleeping with her. At first, I wanted to kill him making up some foolishness like that. But then I saw for myself."

"Saw what?" Prickly hairs rose on my arms. An unexplainable chill made me hold Henry tighter so he wouldn't pull us both over and forward. "What'd you see, mom?"

"I'd gone to her house to see if it was true, if there really was a child. See if she looked anything like Henry or you, or Timothy. We didn't have access to instant DNA tests back then like they do now. I figured if I saw the little girl, I'd know if she was really your father's. Next thing I know, I saw her pour a tiny envelope of powder in a cup of tea she'd offered."

"Sweetener?"

"Yeah, right," she scoffed. "Then I took a look around her place. That's when I started noticing the little statues, wooden figures with names scratched on them. Right then and there, I believed your father. It was the only thing that saved our marriage. Maybe she had drugged him and made him not remember a thing. Or put some kind of hex on him. It would've been the only way I was able to stay with him." Her scowl was hard and deep as if she smelled rotten eggs. "If he'd slept with her on his own volition, unacceptable. I would've had to kill that man in his sleep."

"So you actually believe Dad was drugged?" I was stuck in the middle of the story, the part where the devil made him do it.

"Yes. Absolutely. I saw what she did with my own eyes. I got up out of there, quick and in a hurry, you hear me. I was scared out of my wits. I told Henry if he had anything at all to do with her, he could count me out. That woman was pure evil. I don't know what kind of craziness she was practicing in there, but I saw it with my own eyes."

Mom, a man can't be forced to sleep with someone and spawn a child in the process. That part takes effort if you know what I mean, but I stopped myself from saying this out loud. Essentially she wanted my father's freewill to be absolved from guilt. That way her status of being the most desirable woman in my father's world remained intact.

For the record, mistakes had never been tolerated in the Johnston household. Errors were for sissies. Failures meant you hadn't given your all.

While Lauren and Henry played face squish with each other, I leaned to the side to make sure she saw the truth in what I was about to say. "I'm sorry you had to go through any of this. I know how badly you were hurt. I wish I could make it better, but I can't."

"If you know, then why would you welcome that child into your home?"

I don't have an answer. My blank stare is legendary and my mother hates it. My slip into oblivion is as much a problem for her as her know-it-all determination is for me.

"Well, answer me," she said.

"Mom, the keyword here is child. She's not her mother and neither am I."

****

Bliss heard the voices speaking as if they were coming from the same room. She could hear every word crisp and enunciated. Sometimes she hated her abilities. It wasn't as if she'd lied to Venus earlier. She answered the questions that were asked of her. There was no reason to speak about her other gifts. One of them was hearing other's thoughts. Reading people was as much a curse as it was a blessing. She knew what people were thinking, sometimes even before that person understood his or her own thoughts. Unable to make sense of the haberdashery in their head, Bliss could narrow it down to their fear, hope, or desire in thirty seconds or less. Her mother had the gifts. So did her grandmother, and her mother before her.

In that regard Venus was wrong. We were our mothers. There was no cutting of the circle. It only grew wider and stronger moving onto the next generation. Poor Venus

would never be able to end her attraction to sorrow because it was in her blood. Her mother's blood, filled with
the need for heartache and distraction. But she had other
traits, good ones like being a protector, and honoring her
word. Bliss liked that about Venus the minute they met.
She was also compassionate and honest. Those traits were
rare. She was a good person. Bliss understood that now.

She wouldn't let Pauletta Johnston interfere with her
mission. She pulled out the thick leather book, tattered and
worn, and opened it carefully. Each page was brittle with
use and age.

At one point she'd known this particular prayer by
heart when she'd practiced it all the time. Growing up,
she'd wanted so badly to be liked that she'd find the mean
girl in school and make a new best friend out of her, an
example so to speak. The other kids would see and put her
on a pedestal. As she got older and found peace of mind
she'd walked away from the habit of wanting to be liked.
She stopped cold turkey of fixing other people's percep-
tions and altering their outlooks. Her new found belief
made her understand that what others thought mattered
very little as to how her day, week, or entire life would
unfold. Living in a bubble is what her grandmother called
it. No TV, no Internet, just the two of them thriving off
nature.

But once the vision came, she had no choice. She had to
leave her comfort zone. She hadn't chosen the mission.
"You must save Venus."

How? Exactly what was she supposed to do? Changing someone's mind was different than changing their fate. Last she remembered, changing destinies wasn't part of her skill set.

Bliss read the words before closing her eyes and saying them aloud. By morning there'd be renewal and understanding. So it shall be done.

Opportunity Knocks

The microphone hung overhead picking up all of their conversation. She, Jay, and Christopher were sitting in the restaurant booth like a real family. The cameraman filmed the entire time. Sirena was grateful she'd taken a chunk of her bounty and copped a fresh weave, a salt scrub, and a massage from head to toe. Going on an entire hour in the armpit of a restaurant Christopher had choosen, her hair was still on point and her skin was glowing. She was tingling all over. Part nervousness, part happiness.

They'd eaten dinner and were now waiting for dessert. Christopher ordered a piece of chocolate cake. He hadn't wanted dessert, but she kicked him under the table. She didn't want the evening to end already. Not yet.

When the plate arrived, she leaned over Jake and stuck her fork in the moist gooey treat. "Damn that's good," she cooed. "This is exactly what I needed, Jay, a little one on one family time." She reached again for another scoop.

"So you're liking the word family now, huh? Just add water and stir. I seem to recall you making it sound like a fate worst than death. Suburbia. Children. Marriage. You sure are something, CiCi."

Christopher did the unthinkable and picked up the saucer and placed the entire thing in front of her. "Here, you eat it."

Thank goodness for the camera or she would've plied the thing in the center of his face. Christopher was such a brat. If she hadn't given birth to him, she'd swear he was spawn of the devil himself. But she knew better. Jay was his father so he couldn't be all bad.

"Jay, would you like some?" She played off the rudeness by Christopher best she could.

"Nah, I'm good. Chris, you're not having eat any of this?" Jay said while inching some distance between she and him.

The warm spot she'd coveted minutes earlier was left cold. She felt embarrassed knowing the camera had caught it as well. That's okay, it only proved he still didn't trust himself to be near her.

She turned up her smile and pretended to be unfazed. As many times as she'd been in front of a camera, having one document her every facial expression filled her with anxiety. She knew how to act, how to read lines, how to prepare herself before the camera started rolling. Here it was non-stop. Even when she thought they were letting her take a break, the camera could still be on her, catching that moment where she felt completely vulnerable or broken. Like now, having Jay scoot away from her for the world to see was almost unbearable.

"This has been so much fun. I hope we can do it again soon," she said a few octaves above normal.

"I don't," Christopher lamented. "This sucked. The food was cold. The french fries were stale."

"It's the restaurant you picked," Sirena shrieked, unable to help herself. "Really, Jay, he's spoiled. What're you guys doing over there?"

"None of your business, what we're doing. You're not the boss of me."

Jay cut his eyes at Christopher. "Chris, don't. You know better. That's not what we do." Jay said calmly but the expression on his face spoke volumes. He and Christopher might not have been around each other for long, but enough time to know the, 'boy you better straighten up' look.

Christopher sat up straight. "I thought you said honesty was the best policy?"

"That's right, but you have to know when to use some tact. If you want to get anywhere with the ladies you have to be smooth. You can't just blurt out exactly what's on your mind."

"What's tact?"

"Haven't you heard the saying you get more with honey than with vinegar?"

"No. Besides, I don't want anything from her."

Sirena couldn't help it, she was dismantled. The eleven year old was taking her apart in front of the world. Or at least he would be once it aired and people saw the disrespectful little tyrant in action. Then again, maybe they'd see what she was up against and feel sorry for her. For a split second she wondered if her assassin would give her a two for the price of one special. Life would be easier without both he and Venus, but then again, Christopher was the glue holding this project together. Without him, Jay would have no reason to have her in his life.

She took a moment to gather herself. Besides, it wasn't Christopher's fault if his daddy didn't know a good thing right in front of him. Sirena had watched the previous episodes of *Distinguished Gentleman* and gotten angry wondering why Jay would settle for less when he could've had an A-list chic by his side. They were a magic duo, everyone said so. All the movie reviewers made a special point to talk about their magnetic chemistry on screen. Not to mention their infallible music together. She got goose bumps just thinking about their future as a powerhouse duo.

"Christopher, why don't you go sit in the car and let me and Jay enjoy dessert, in private?"

Christopher raised his eyebrows at Jay. "Can I?" he saw light at the end of this dismal tunnel. "Please?"

"It's night time. I'm not comfortable letting you out of my sight."

"I rather sit in the car. Please," he begged.

Jay pulled the car keys out of his pocket. "Don't talk to anyone. Sit in the backseat. Do not touch the gears. Lock the doors as soon as you get inside and text me. I'll be out there in twenty minutes."

"Gah, I'm not seven years old." He shoved one of the fries into his mouth for good measure.

"Thought they were stale," she mimicked. She was truly relieved when he was gone. She didn't know how she was going to pull off motherhood. The wife part she could do no problem, but taking on Christopher without putting a fist upside his head was going to be a job in overtime.

"I'm glad we're alone. There's so much I want to talk to you about." Sirena was feeling her moment. She could almost feel the camera zoom in on her face. She made sure there were budding tears. "It really pains me to talk about this, but I'm about to lose my house and everything I've worked so hard for." She spoke as if it were a secret but just that morning one of those rude disgusting gossip sites had gotten a hold of the court documents and posted them for the world to see. She couldn't believe how easy it was for those people to find out anything and everything about a person. There was no privacy left in the world.

Jay sat in silence with a blank stare obviously feeling like she'd put him on the spot.

She leaned in closer. "No. You think I'm asking for money? I'd never do that. But what you can do is write me a hit song. Think about it, you and me in a studio doing what we do best. What are waiting for? If not now, when? That's the only way I'm going to get out of this mess. If I lose my house, then what, I'll have to come live with you and your wife in that big old mansion of yours," she said with a chuckle so he'd think she was only joking.

The real deal was that he knew she wasn't joking. He had her son in his possession. Somehow he had to connect the dots and know that she wasn't going to disappear.

She'd signed adoption papers a mere six months ago and he knew as well as she how much time she had left to rescind them. Her problems would be his problems as long as Christopher was the link between them.

He swallowed hard. "I don't know, you think I can throw something together and then, bam instant hit?" He was under pressure. *Distinguished Gentleman* was all about his ability to leap tall buildings with a single bound, take care of those around him, and make it all look easy breezy in the process. Could he be callous enough to say No to the mother of his son and sit idly by as she lost her home. "Please, Jay. If anyone can save me, it's you."

He was her hero, she gloated to herself, always had been, and regardless of what he or wifey thought about it, he always would be.

"Alright. I'll put a few beats together. This time, you write the lyrics," he said, as if the obligation was killing him.

"Jacob Parson, no one will ever be as good to me as you are." If she could've yelled 'cut' she would have. It was the perfect segue to their future.

Says Who Says You

Jake came home very late and I couldn't wait to tell him I was sorry for the earlier drama. It was one of those days I was glad was over. At least I thought it was over. After the fainting scare I had earlier all I wanted to do was show my appreciation for life.

What if the last time I saw my husband we'd been fighting? I didn't want to be at war anymore. I was determined to make it up to Jake. I'd even found a nice teddy that fit well enough. My breast spilled out the center. The elastic casing felt like fiberglass around my torso. I figured he would have me out of it quick enough once I made it clear I no longer cared about camera and such. I was ready to suck up my dignity for the sake of love. But in he walked with that woman's name in his mouth.

"I think you're right. Sirena is up to no good," he said walking right past my sweetness all on display. "Do you know she had the nerve to talk on camera about her house going into foreclosure. She even made it a point to ask me if we could work together because if we didn't, it would be up to us to take care of her. After all the mess she's put us through."

So that's where Darcie and her camera crew had been. I ignored the little angry bird on my shoulder. I wasn't going to let Sirena win especially when she wasn't even in the room. I heard the shower turn on. I scooted out of bed and slipped my feet into the inch high gold mules on standby for this kind of emergency.

"You mind if I join you?" I sucked in my tummy and pushed out the offerings.

Finally, he noticed. "Wow, baby. You look amazing." He reached into the shower and twisted the chrome knob until the water stopped.

"I bet I taste even better," I said softly. It was a bold move. He flicked off the lights. I flicked them back on. If there were cameras I'd rather there be a triple rating too graphic for television.

Without warning I was plastered against the open door. Jake's firm hands slipped underneath the thin fabric and led the way. I was wet and waiting. He moaned his appreciation and took his seat at the dinner table. A three course meal topped off with dessert. I tried to put a muzzle on myself, covering my mouth with my hand. But there was no way to tone down the eruption about to take place. If orgasms had names this one would be called the Tsunami. Or the Great Wall of some place in a far distant land. Every tingling fiber in my body began to explode. I clambered to stay upright to no avail. I eventually slid floor level exactly where Jake wanted me.

There was nothing left of my lace dainties. Straps broken, fabric barely holding together. Jake seemed insatiable. He held me tight later in bed and whispered, "Thank you," in my ear. "I needed that."

"You and me both," I said against his chest. "Today was something for the books I really wanted to say I was sorry for not hearing you this morning. I know you think I'm beautiful. I feel it in your touch, in your kiss."

"All right now. You might be asking for more trouble."

I took his hand that was getting too happy and brought it to my face. "Tell me what happened today."

"He choked out a nervous laugh. "You go first."

"Well, um, we have another guest."

"Who?"

"My mom's here."

"Seriously?"

"Yes. She got on a plane, caught a taxi, and now she's in the room down the hall. What a day."

"I'm even more impressed."

"Me too. She came here all by herself."

"No. I mean impressed that you let me sex you up with your mom a couple of doors away." His hand eased across my chin. He leaned in for a kiss. "Tomorrow, I'm going straight to the mall and pick you up a couple more of those lace numbers."

"Oh stop. I can't believe I was such a freak."

"Very impressive," He said again, this time grinning ear to ear.

"Your turn. The dinner with Christopher and Sirena? Spill it."

His grin disappeared. His face turned sullen. "Okay. Everything went pretty much as planned. Here's the thing..." His words turned into a trail of garbled sentences.

Surely, I was hearing things. "Wait a minute, did you just say, you're going to be working with Sirena?"

"It's either that, or..." Jake pulled my hand off his neck where I'd used the claw grip.

"She's having a hard time. She's not working. No one will give her a shot. Her reputation is trashed. She's got nothing better to do than drive you and me crazy."

I wasn't falling for it. "So did she even talk to Christopher or was this all about her usual manipulation?"

His expression gave me the answer. "That's pitiful. She's truly pitiful. So you're actually letting her win by agreeing to work with her. Can't you see this is like feeding the kitty cat milk and expecting her to go away? We're never going to be rid of her if you keep falling for her lies."

"She's about to lose her house. That's not a lie. No one will hire her. That's not a lie. If I don't help her get back on track, she's going to be dangerous."

"Dangerous, how? I'm sick of her threatening you every time she needs attention. So what now, is she threatening to take Christopher? She signed away her rights, you know. We don't have to be afraid of her anymore."

"None of that stuff is written in stone, you know that."

I bit down plucking a nice chunk of my inner cheek. A nervous habit. I wanted to take a bite out of Sirena. "She's like a virus. I wish she'd just disappear." If anyone was counting how many times I'd made that wish, it would've already come true.

"Me too. But that's not going to happen." Jake's dark lashes closed over his eyes. "One more thing."

"No. I'm not listening to you." I covered my ears for dramatic effect. Everyone knew you could still hear whether you wanted to or not.

"Darcie signed her on for a couple of episodes on the show."

I could feel the steam rising. I was going to pop.

"It's going to work out to our advantage," he said, feeling all confident and master of the universe-ish. "Any publicity is good publicity. We've only got three more weeks of filming. A couple of scenes with us in the studio, and that's it."

"Are you saying you plan to include her in the show, write her a hit record, and then expect her to go away, and you call me naive." I shook my head with disgust when all he could do was hunch his shoulders. If I were counting, this would be the third night in a row going to bed angry, something I didn't want to do. I could solve that problem. I scooted out of the bed, slipped on my robe, and snatched my pillow he had somehow made his. "I'm going to sleep downstairs. The air is better down there."

"Babe. Don't go. I promise this is going to work out."

I moved with lightning speed out the door.

My name is Venus Parson and I'm in Love with Jake Parson, but I refused to let him make a fool of me with Sirena Lassiter and her failing career and self-grandeur. I had my limits.

Forget about my problems. I was on my own. Not like it was the first time. Fine, I'd figure everything out myself. I didn't need him anyway.

Sticks, Stones, and Shaken Bones

I was jittery from not having slept more than a couple of hours worrying about how the face to face meeting was going to go with my mom and Bliss. I'd also spent the night gnashing my teeth over the news of Jake and Sirena working together in the studio. It was all I could do not to yank Darcie by the ear that morning and ask if she was trying to destroy our marriage or was it just a hazard of the producer's job.

Suggesting Sirena be a part of the show gave new meaning to poisoning the well. But then I remembered who was really responsible. This wasn't new behavior. Jake had let Sirena into our lives once before resulting in our separation for a short time. All because of his inability to say no to her. I didn't want Sirena to know how much she got under my skin. It was best I pretended she didn't exist.

It was a fact, the more you resisted something, the bigger it grew in power. I refused to give her anymore power. I kissed Jake in the morning for the camera. I smiled and waved the kids off to school. Besides, I had to focus on my mother for the next few days. Hopefully she wouldn't stay longer than that.

I made reservations for three at the Briar Patch café for Bliss, my mother, and me. From the surface we looked like three ladies out for a casual lunch. If not for my mother's brooding frown we'd also look like we were happy to be there.

"So here we are," I clasped my hands together.

I had low hopes for the meeting going well. If I didn't expect too much, any results would be great. But I knew for sure my mother was never going to accept Bliss. The best I could do was have a forced intervention in a public place.

The camera pointed in our direction was only a small distraction to the other restaurant patrons. When they were told we were taping a reality show, a universal 'oh right' circled the room. What city didn't have a reality show filming in their town? It was almost common place to see a camera following someone these days.

"You look exactly like your mother," Pauletta said to Bliss. "Nothing like my husband."

Okay, here we go.

"Really? The minute I saw Venus, I thought we kind of looked alike." Bliss scooted a bit closer and placed her face against mine almost taunting my mother.

"No. I don't see it at all," Pauletta said with a bland expression. "Which brings me to my suggestion. You should consider having a DNA test? It would be a shame for you to two to spend all this time building a relationship, and then find out you're not really related."

"Yes, it would be a shame," I said evenly. "That would mean there was another woman out there who was really my sister, and we'd have to go through this all over again. I'd rather keep this one." I smiled at Bliss.

"Oh for heaven's sake." My mother fluttered her eyes. "Why am I here? You've obviously picked which side of the fence you're on."

"Mom, I'm not going to be in the middle of whatever happened thirty years ago between you and dad. That's something you have to deal with. I'm not here to pick sides. I don't think it's too much to ask that you respect my choice to accept Bliss."

"Fine."

"Okay. Then, we're off to a good start."

Bliss let her chin rest on her clasped fingers as if she could care less how the afternoon went. She wasn't affected by my mother's disdain one bit. I wished I had her temperament and didn't wear my emotions on my sleeve.

"I understand your family, your mother's side was from a Latin country," Pauletta questioned with the skill of a journalist. I'd never seen her this tactful in her sleuthing skills. Normally she just fired away and didn't care whether she hit her mark or missed it entirely.

"My mother's parents, my grandmother and grandfather were originally from Haiti."

I felt a nudge. My mother's foot. No doubt this concluded her assumptions. Bliss's mother was some Santeria practicing vixen that shook tiny animal bones in a wooden cup before wishing a curse on her enemy.

"I would like to make a toast to new beginnings." I raised my Perrier with a twist of lime while my mother lifted a cup of green tea, and for Bliss a glass of red wine.

"To new beginnings," Bliss repeated. "I'm so happy you've included me. Really, Mrs. Johnston, I've always wished I could be a part of your family.

"Ahuh, yeah, well..." Pauletta was gunning up for the kill. But before she could pull out her sharpened blades, Bliss interrupted and reached across the table. She let a slender hand fall on my mother's wrist. The earth didn't shatter. My mother left her hand in place, and didn't pull away.

"This has been a dream come true finding my sister. Venus has welcomed me. We have an instant connection. I love my nieces and nephews. This has all been too cool. I'm glad you have finally accepted me too. Thank you, Pauletta."

"You're welcome." Her lips parted in a semi-smile, yet genuine.

I nearly spit up my water. Either Pauletta Johnston had missed her calling as an actress or she actually had a miraculous change of mind, body, and spirit.

My mother spoke slowly. "You are a welcome addition. I can't believe we had to wait this long to have you in our family."

I gulped the ball of incredibility down my throat. I'm telling myself this is real. This is happening, but I still don't quite believe it.

"It would be nice if you visited me and Henry in Los Angeles. He would love to see you. I just know it's just what this family needs to heal."

I tried to keep my face from bursting in a state of shock. Even Darcie seemed perplexed. She'd wanted fireworks. A bit more neck dragging and eye rolling. This was too cordial and sophisticated.

"I'm feeling the love in the room. How about we order something to eat and get this party started," my mother said with a new brightness to her tone.

"Well, look who's here?" The undeniable voice of Sirena landed like a dagger in my back.

The cameraman and the sound tech turned their focus on Sirena. Darcie smiled with relief as if they'd worked her arrival down to perfection. Just in time to save this snooze fest.

Sirena stood towering over us wearing strapless denim dress completely over accessorized with the belt, shoes, and earrings like she'd hijacked a Bloomingdale's dummy.

"You must be Jay's mother-in-law. I've heard so much about you." Sirena pulled her tomato red lips into a clown smile while laying a hand on my mother's shoulder.

"And you must be...I'm sorry, I don't recognize you." My mother's eyes darted to where she was being touched signifying that if Sirena wanted to keep her limb, she should move it, and quickly. That was the reaction I'd expected earlier when Bliss did the same thing. All this hand laying was starting to scare me. Some kind of body snatching sci-fi thing was happening.

"Such a small world," Sirena announced. "I'd planned on meeting a friend here but she canceled. Would you mind if I joined you? Doesn't look like anyone's ordered yet."

Only then did I see the mic already hooked around Sirena's back. Just like I thought, this was a set-up. I smiled for the camera but I was sure my nostrils were blowing out smoke. "Actually, we did order. Sorry." I did my best to keep my breathing under control.

"I'm sure they wouldn't mind putting in an additional plate." She kept her gaze on me waiting for a reaction.

I kept my vow not to let her see me upset. "You know what, Sirena, have a seat. It would be nice to have you join us."

"Oh, you're Sirena," Pauletta announced between a loud sip of her tea. "The one who pretended Christopher was her little brother. So nice to finally meet you."

Sirena hesitated, not sure how to respond to the jab. "Nice to meet you too." She decided to ignore it. Good decision. She scooted herself in.

"And this is my sister Bliss, you met her the other day."

"Yes, hello." Sirena barely looked in her direction.

"Pauletta, will you split a salad with me? I'm not that hungry." Bliss tapped my mother's hand to get her attention. "What do you say?" She let the question linger gently in the air. An almost imperceptible shift, but I saw it. My mother's eyes went sharp and icy.

"I say there is no reason I should have to have lunch with his hussy? I didn't sign on for this, no sir-eee."

"Okay, that's just a bit rude," Sirena said, shifting her attention between Darcie and my mother. Obviously, she hadn't signed on for this either.

"Rude?" Pauletta fired back. "I mean really, you didn't care a thing about my daughter when you were trying to steal her husband. Man thief that's what you are."

"Mom. Stop it," I snapped but it was as if she was hypnotized to say absolutely everything on the tip of her tongue...or someone else's. I looked over at Bliss who had a sly but demure smile on her face. Her eyes glistened with intensity.

"So tell me, are there any more offspring we should know about?" Pauletta asked. "You wouldn't have a baby sister who happens to be your daughter too, would you?"

Sirena turned her eyes on me.

I raised my hands in innocence. "Hey, leave me out of this."

She stood up. "I can see you and your mother have spent a lot time talking about me. Didn't know I meant so much to you."

"Trust me, you do not." It was happening again. My head was pounding. I could hear the surge of blood rushing past my ears. I looked up at Sirena and there were two of her. I dropped my eyes right before her red lips tightened ready to say something else but thought better of it. All I could think was if looks could kill. She turned and left zigzagging her way around tables.

"Glad you got the hint," Pauletta called after her. "The nerve. Crashing our lunch like that. You may put up with that little tramp, but not me. Life is too short."

"I couldn't have said it better," Bliss said with a wink. She turned to me. "Are you okay?"

"Yeah, I'm fine," I lied. My stomach was in a knot. My vision was blurred and I could barely hold the glass of water. "I think we should leave," I said, ignoring Darcie's disappointment.

She swirled a finger in the air for the camera crew to stop filming. She leaned over my shoulder. "We need at least twenty more minutes on film. Can you do that?"

"No. I'm sorry. Maybe you can chase down Sirena. She's still wearing the microphone you hooked up to her." I unhooked mine and left it on the table.

Back home we all went our separate ways. I retreated to my bedroom dazed and confused. I welcomed the moments replaying in my head, determined to understand what just happened. My mother had been under some kind of spell. There was no other way to explain it.

I picked up my phone to call Jake. He was filming a commercial for a new sports drink. He of course credited Distinguished Gentleman for the opportunity. Just like Keisha had predicted. The show was going to keep him in the spotlight long enough to bring in better offers. But that's not why I hung up before the phone began to ring. I couldn't tell him what I'd witnessed at lunch. The cruel dichotomy was that I had no one else to tell. He was my best friend, but also ready, if there was one false move, to pull the trigger on Bliss.

"Okay. Relax. I can get to the bottom of this," I told myself. "I will handle everything." I knew exactly who to call.

Before I entered the kitchen, I heard a melody of voices. Bliss was holding Mya's hand and I immediately panicked. What if she touched Mya and turned her into a raving lunatic like she did my mother.

"Introducing the lovely Mya wearing a stunning ensemble." Mya did a twitch of her seven year old hips and a full model's turn. I clapped nervously while my mother cheered.

"Work it, girlfriend." Pauletta offered two snaps and a head nod. "I can't believe how fast my first grandbaby has grown up." Pauletta leaned in for a kiss. "Who made your hair so pretty?"

"Aunt Bliss did it." Mya ran her hand down her braid that was no different than how I did her hair almost every single day for school. The only difference was the silk flower pinned near her ear.

"You're a lucky girl to have such a gifted auntie who can make your hair so pretty."

The crazy lovefest between Pauletta and Bliss was getting scarier by the moment. I jingled my car keys. "I have to make a run. You guys going to be all right."

"We'll be fine," my mother chimed.

I needed to get out of there, get some air so I could think everything through.

Not to mention I needed to call my father back so he could stop worrying. He'd already called twice and each time I was afraid to answer around my mother. The least I could do was call and confirm there was peace through out the land. I definitely wouldn't be making it up.

"Seriously?" he questioned my report.

I drove while I talked. His voice came over the Bluetooth nice and clear. Not like when we were both usually whispering afraid of Pauletta's wrath.

"Yes. They're getting along fabulously. You see no worries."

"I just knew things were going to get ugly."

"Well, I thought the same thing. But you know what they say about assumptions. Since everyone's getting along, now you can come visit too. The more the merrier is my motto."

"I'll call back and check on you," was the best he could offer.

"Okay, dad. I love you."

"Love you too, Precious."

I hung up still feeling like I had no one to talk to though I'd just finished talking to my dad. I pulled the car off the exit hoping I wasn't wrong about the one person who would listen and understand.

In Bloom

The floral shop was doing well. Seeing the sign hanging over the building always gave me a rush of pride. I'd started the business a few years earlier. Trevelle and Vince were doing a great job running it. I'd officially sold it to Vince after I was put on bed rest in the sixth month of pregnancy with the twins. I knew I wouldn't have the time or energy to run the place. Vince loved the flower business probably more than me. No one would guess it to be true with his alpha male exterior and no nonsense approach, but the man knew how to put together the most beautiful arrangements.

"Hello, anyone here?"

"Well look at you, gorgeous." Vince came from the back and rushed forward with a hug easily lifting me off the ground. I guess I wasn't as big as I felt half the time.

I was still wearing the high heels and dress from the lunch date earlier. The fact that I could zip it up made me proud, but hearing Vince call me gorgeous added a new level of happy on my face.

He took my hand. "Come here. Want to show you something."

I followed him to the work room. He pulled open a drawer and took out a thick black photo album. "One of the brides dropped this off. She was so happy with the work we did, she had the photographer put together an entire album just for the store."

I sat down and flipped the thick pages. "Wow, Vince. These are beautiful. You've stepped it up, I see."

"Actually Trevelle did most the designs in that package."

"Nice. Very nice. Speaking of Trevelle, where is she? I'd love to see her."

His eyebrow raised in suspicion. "Really?"

"Vince, we've been on good terms for a while now. You know that. All that drama is so last year." Admittedly, his new wife, my old nemesis, had been a bitter enemy at one time. Her habit for falling in love with the men in my life had nothing to do with it.

Seemed like a million years ago when she was married to my ex-boyfriend, Airic Fisher, who was the sperm-donor of Mya. He'd never wanted anything to do with Mya until Trevelle came along and convinced him to fight me for custody. As the queen madam of TV evangelists, she wasn't about to be married to a man who wasn't taking responsibility for his own child.

After an exhaustive battle in court, Jake and I finally won. Trevelle eventually apologized, and admitted she had only been acting on the pain of losing her own daughter at birth. If anyone understood that kind of loss, it was me. We weren't best friends, but we'd certainly buried the hatchet.

Vince folded his arms across his body builder chest. "Okay, spill it. What's going on?"

"If it was something I wanted to talk to you about, I wouldn't be looking for your other half. It's girl stuff," I said with a dismissive hand flip.

"Girl stuff?"

"Why do you repeat everything I say like you don't believe me?"

This time it was both eyebrows raised.

"Vince, all that drama with me and Trevelle is so far under the bridge. You know that. I think it's sweet you're so protective, but I just want to talk to her."

It's not like he actually saw me try to claw her eyes out or rip out her extensions. All hearsay.

"Okay. I believe you. She's in school. She's taking classes."

My eyes bugged out. "School?"

"Now who's repeating everything?" He mimicked with wiggle of his head.

"I believe you." Something in my expression gave me away.

"You're never too old to go back to school. I'm surprised you'd even think like that."

"No. You're right. I know. What's she studying?"

"Holistic healing."

"I thought she already knew how to heal? All those years touching people's foreheads and then they miraculously rose up from the their wheelchairs."

"Stop that."

"Sorry," I said. "I just need to talk to her. What's her schedule? Will she be back in like the next thirty minutes?"

Vince shook his head, no. "When she gets back I'll tell her to call you."

"No. Tell her to come over."

"I will give her the message. But you're sure you don't want Uncle Vince to weigh in. You know I've got all the answers."

I stood up and gave him a pat on the back with my goodbye hug. "Not this time. Girl stuff," I reminded him. "But you're welcome to come. I've been meaning to have you two over for dinner."

He leaned back to read my face. "That would be nice. I may take you up on that. I haven't seen my God babies since they were a couple of weeks old."

"So there you go, it's a date."

The Company We Keep

"Have I told you how good you look, babe? You're working that dress." Jake stood next to me while I tossed the salad. I worked diligently. I hadn't said much to him since he'd come home. It was safer that way. Once I got comfortable there'd be no stopping me from singing like a canary.

"Can you get me the olive oil?"

"If you give a kiss first." He puckered up, enjoying the game of silence.

I avoided his lips and turned my cheek.

"Fine, I'll get it myself."

"Okay, how long is this going to go on?" He asked, darting his eyes to let me know we weren't alone.

The cameraman had a perfect angle over his shoulder. I had no choice but to ease my stance. The worst thing I could do was let the world see me being mean to the great JP. There'd be an uprising from his fans. Twitter-verse would put out a hit on me.

"I'm just trying to get this done. Trevelle and Vince will be here in twenty minutes. So, help or move along."

He pulled out the wine glasses and set them on the table. He knew the drill for a dinner party. He opened up the drawer and grabbed the silverware. "I'm happy to help. But where are your mother and sister?"

"They are my guests. I'm the one entertaining. And weren't you the one making specific requests about who cooked what in the Parson household."

"Just asking, babe." He didn't want me to go any further with that line of conversation.

I pulled the roast out of the oven and checked it with a fork. Tender and juicy. I hadn't made a roast in years, but it came out exactly like my mother used to make. "All right, everything is done."

I checked the table setting. Jake knew better than I where the silverware went for formal dining. Something I could never remember.

Jake wrapped is arms around me from behind. "Do you need me to do anything else?"

"You can check on the kids, make sure everyone is tucked in and happy so we won't be interrupted during dinner."

"Your wish is my command."

He was doing his best to be helpful, but I felt like he was in the way. I had one thing on my mind and that was getting Trevelle within touching distance of Bliss. I expected the two of them would clash in a storm of wills. But the results would be the most telling. If Trevelle suddenly turned demure and full of accolades, I'd know who was the stronger of the bunch.

The doorbell rang. Jake went to get the door. I followed closely right behind him, excited to have my guest finally arrive.

Vince and Trevelle arrived promptly at seven. Shelly was sent in with her clipboard to get signatures. "What's this," Vince asked.

"It's a release giving us permission to film you."

"The show, honey. Remember Distinguished Gentleman," Trevelle cheesed, ready for her close up. She'd already signed her copy and handed it back to Shelly.

"That's not going to work out for me," Vince slid his hands in his black denim jeans. "I can't sign that."

"Sweetheart, it's nothing serious." Trevelle put out her spindly fingers. She took the clipboard and read the gist of it. "You give them permission to use your likeness in the filming and do not hold them liable for any misrepresentation. Pretty straight forward and simple. Sign." She pushed it toward him.

"Can't do it," Vince said shaking his head.

"It's okay. You know what. I'll just tell them they can't film. I want you here, Vince."

Jake came down the stairs from checking on the kids in time to hear the not filming part. "What's going on?"

"Vince isn't comfortable with the cameras at the dinner table. And I agree. We should be able to have a nice dinner with friends without the world watching."

"I can respect that. No problem. We'll just ask them to leave." Jake put out a hand and gave Vince a man hug.

"Wait a minute. Why is it such a big deal?" Trevelle asked. "Vince, it's a reality show, hun. They're just cameras filming a nice dinner party. I don't understand."

I always had a feeling the life Vince led before this one was on the wrong side of the law. He refused to talk about it. He made it clear anytime I pried that he did some bad things that he wasn't proud of, and left it at that. Hearing Trevelle's confusion made me understand he hadn't shared his secret with her either. Man and wife and still there were secrets. None of us were immune.

"Trevelle, really, it's not a problem."

"It is a problem. Some of us aren't afraid to shine. I'd like a few minutes in front of the camera. Why would you deny me that? You knew I was getting dressed and putting extra effort into my make-up. What, did you think I was doing it for, just to see Venus and Jake? No offense, Venus."

"None taken."

"I'm sorry, doll. You know I'd do it if I could. I'd do anything for you."

"Apparently not."

"Trevelle, I have an idea, why don't you come over tomorrow and we'll have a full day. You can stay as long as you like while we film."

"How am I going to ever get my ministry back if my shine is being blocked? Doesn't matter when the time presents itself if my own husband is camera shy. I know my time is coming. Did you really think I wanted to be holed up in that flower shop for the next twenty years? How are you going to be my helpmate and you want to hide?"

"I know, doll. I know." His Sicilian toned skin was beginning to turn a deep shade of red.

Jake led the way past us. Darcie and the camera crew followed. He opened the door for them. "I really appreciate you guys understanding," he said as they filed out. After the last person left, he closed the door and smacked his hands together. "All right. Let's eat. That food is calling my name."

Trevelle's face filled with regret. She straightened out her St. John jacket. "I'm sorry. I apologize for being so harsh. I shouldn't have gone on that way."

"I understand. It's okay. Let's just go the dining room and have a nice dinner. I'll go get my mother and my sister. I'm excited for you to meet her." Most excited. That's what this meeting was all about. I needed Trevelle, the master of spirituality, to be in the same room as Bliss. Surely, she'd sense some kind of higher power.

"I'm sorry, I'm way too upset. I don't want to be a downer on your dinner party. I think we'll be going."

"Trevelle, no. Please, stay."

But it was already too late. She was out the door. Vince leaned in and hugged me.

"I'm really sorry about that." It was the saddest I'd ever seen him look.

"Vince, it's okay. I completely understand." I touched his face that suddenly had stubble. After a quick hug, he was out the door too.

Jake closed it behind him. "Wow. That was crazy, huh?"

"Secrets. That's what this was about. He can't tell her his secrets," I swallowed back the tears that threatened to come. "Why are secrets necessary? What about us? Is there something you want to tell me, anything?" I waited, hoping the answer was no.

"Babe, no. I gave that up a long time ago. I never want to keep secrets from you."

"Wanting and doing are two different things."

"Just like last night when I came home and told you everything, even though I knew you'd be pissed. No secrets." He pressed a soft kiss on my forehead. "Call your mother and Bliss down. I will even serve you ladies. Come on. Let's go have this amazing dinner."

Best Laid Plans

Sirena entered the circular paved entry of her house, at least hers for the next couple of months. The weeds were knee high throughout the yard. The fountain was dry and filled with debris. The gardener and pool guy had been the first to go when the money started running low.

She was counting down until the day the Sherriff showed up to move her out. Her goal was to move before that happened. If the gossip sites got a report of that gem she'd never live it down.

She parked in the front not bothering to use the garage. Who cared if the sun faded the paint of the over priced vehicle. It wasn't going to be her car that much longer. Soon she'd have to drive the gas guzzling SUV that was still parked in her garage, the one her cousin used as her bodyguard. Those were the good old days.

She could almost picture the limos, Jags, and Mercedes, lined up in the turnstile when she'd thrown a get together. Reminiscing about the parties and friends hanging out only made her regret her choice of girlfriends. Like the hired workers, they too left when the money ran out.

All of this just because she played big sister instead of mommy. As if her choice had anything to do with her talent. She'd sold well over five million records. Made movies that the studios profited on big time. Now they wouldn't touch her with a 10-foot pole.

She tossed her keys on the granite tabletop at the entry and marveled at the echo of the simplest movement. Her steps throughout the hall sounded like she was in a cathedral.

The place was close to empty. She'd sold the baby grand piano, the art, rugs, and most of the furniture one piece at a time. All that was left was her bedroom furnishings. She took off her high heels before taking the stairs.

Her hand traced the spiral staircase. Truly a work of art. If she could figure out how to unhinge the wrought iron she'd sell that too. But then how would she get to her bed, which was calling her name?

She dived in the thousand-count sheets face first. Sleeping the day away until her knight rescued her had become a bad habit. Like Rapunzel she awaited her handsome prince to call out her name so she could throw her long wavy locks out the window for him to climb his way up.

Yes, Jay, save me. He tugged at the long trail of hair to make sure it didn't give out on him. This made her head jerk back. Another tug and surely it would separate from her scalp. Wait, she moaned in her sleep, as the pain grew too real. The tugging too real. She struggled to get free, flailing at the air. Now it seemed the hair had become her enemy, wrapping itself around her neck and pulling tight.

If only she could be free of the grip closing on her windpipe. She would be able to scream for help.

She finally cried out. She sat up in bed. Her heart was beating out of her chest. She felt around her neck. She pushed herself out of the bed and fumbled her way to the bathroom. She found the light, switched it on and was horrified to see herself in the mirror. There were scratches. Whelps were growing by the second. The skin underneath her nails, the fine claw marks going in one downward direction told her the red marks had come from her own doing. Just a bad dream, she told herself.

But so real.

She ran the water and patted the sting with the coolness. Get it together. It's not like she'd ever done drugs. She drank every now and then, but not enough for hallucinating and dreaming like a wild woman.

Back in bed she shivered with fear. Afraid to fall asleep again. The phone she held in her palm began to ring. She didn't recognize the number but she took a chance and answered anyway. The bill collectors usually didn't call so late in the evening.

"Hello," she answered bravely, though shaken. Even talking to a rude collection agent was better than the noise of her own thoughts.

"Miss Sanborne, I need to speak with you. We need to meet," the familiar man's voice ordered.

She cut him off before he could go any further. "I don't have anymore money."

"I'm not interested in more money. We need to meet, tonight."

Sirena checked the time. Nine o'clock and the sun had long set. Her wild dreams made her not want to be out after dark. She certainly didn't want to leave and then have to come back to her big empty house. She'd rather be securely locked in with the alarm set even if it was only good for the noise. The monthly payment to the dispatch service was yet another thing discontinued.

"Put it this way, you have no choice," he said. "Not if you want this thing to happen, and soon."

Sirena filled her cheeks with air and blew out coolly. "Why can't you just deliver? Why?"

"I think it'd be wise not to say more over the phone," his tone went low and threatening.

"This is the last time." She hung up and got out of bed. She changed into a black turtleneck and threw on a pair of jeans. She dressed quickly using her tussled hair to cover the scratches she'd inflicted on herself.

On her way out, she grabbed her keys and pulled the heavy door open. A man was standing there. Not once had she gotten a good look at her assassin but knew instantly that it was him. When she tried to close the door he shoved it open and came inside, locking it behind him.

"How did you know where I live?" She put her arms out to keep a safe distance.

"I wasn't absolutely sure until you opened the door." He grinned with a perfect set of teeth. He wore sunglasses though it was already dark outside. His blazer, jeans, and black expensive loafers hardly looked like he'd come to kill her but she backed up anyway.

"What are you doing here?" She took a few more steps away from him while deciding which way she should run.

"I'm not here to hurt you."

"Oh really? That's news."

"I'm not a violent man. I outsource. Much more effective." He slipped his hand into his jacket pocket.

Sirena ducked, afraid he was coming out with a gun, or a knife.

It was a white envelope. Her envelope. "We have to talk about your deposit."

"I'm done paying you."

"Hardly. In fact, you've only just begun, Sirena. And this little amount doesn't do it justice. Once I figured out who you really were, I knew I'd underbid the job." He tossed it to her feet.

Sirena swallowed hard. "Seriously. Does it look like I'm in any position to pay you more money? Look around you. What do you see? Nothing. That's what."

For a second or two he seemed to realize what she was saying. He bowed his head. "People like you always have a secret stash. Off shore account or two? I know you have something and if this is as important to you as it sounds, you'll find another fifty grand."

Sirena nearly choked on the ridiculousness of it all. She did her best not to fall out in a fit of giggles. Her eyes watered from trying to stifle her laughter. "Oh man. You're way off base. If you're such a great private detective, how come you don't know where this so-called secret stash is? And when you find it, give me some." She threw up her hands. "Guess you're gonna have to call it off, cause I don't have another dime to give you." She picked up the envelope. "Or maybe I can find someone who will do it. Thanks for the refund."

He took off his sunglasses. His dark eyes fixed sharply in her direction. To her surprise he wasn't bad looking like you'd expect a criminal, psychopathic murderer for hire to look. "There are other ways to pay," he said slowly. He leaned forward and took one step at a time. She moved until she backed herself against the wall. He ran his hand down the front of her sweater, played with the strands of her hair before pushing them out of the way.

"Wait a minute," he said shocked at the red welts on her chin and neck. "You all right?"

She shoved him in his chest. "Get the hell out of my house."

"Fine." He snatched the envelope out of her hand. "I'll just keep this for my troubles. But the job will be called off."

"Wait," Sirena shouted. "Just wait a minute." She rushed toward him angry and desperate. He turned around to defend himself and was shocked when she kissed him hard pushing her tongue in the center of his mouth. "This what you want?" She whispered under his chin. "Is this what you want?" She unzipped his jeans and stuck her hand into the opening. She had a firm grip of more than she bargained for. He grabbed her with both hands and picked her up. Her legs straddled him as he carried her up the stairs, but they only made it midway.

He yanked off her jeans and groaned appreciation.

"No. Not without a condom," she panted under her breath. She was surprised that she needed him as much as he needed to have her. He reached into the jean pockets that were now around his ankles and pulled out the shiny package. "You do the honors."

The stairs railed against her back as he drove himself deep and hard inside of her. She twisted and writhed, savoring each thrust. Now it was his turn asking the questions. "Is this what you want, huh?"

By the time it was over, she was barely able to hold up her head. He pushed himself off of her and stumbled up the rest of the way of the stairs. She listened as he took heavy steps to her bathroom. The toilet flushed. She thought she was hearing things when the shower turned on. Heavy footsteps again. He was standing over her. He put out his hand. "Get up."

He practically carried her since she could barely walk. He held her up and pulled open the shower door. He pulled off her last piece of clothing, her tangled sweater over her head and told her to get in. The water was the perfect temperature. He stepped inside right behind her, shoved her fully under the pulse of the showerhead and began to kiss her again, far more gentle this time.

He squeezed soap into the soft sponge and rubbed her back gently. She winced and cried out. There must've been friction burns from the stairs. He turned the water cooler then kissed her moist shoulder as the water poured over her body. "Don't worry. I got you. I'm going to take care of you from now on."

Forever Hold Your Peace

"Unzip me so I can breathe," I told Jake. I kicked off my high heels and relaxed for the first time all day.

"Oh my goodness." He pressed up against me while he did the honors. I felt his hardness grow between our bodies. He slipped in a kiss on the back of my neck.

"Thank you. I need to go feed the twins." I headed to the closet to find something more comfortable to wear. More like my oversized sweatpants with the drawstring and my USC Alma mater T-shirt

Jake followed and cornered me. "Henry and Lauren are sleep. I checked on them like five minutes ago."

"Fine. I guess that leaves time for me to get some rest."

"Okay. Okay," he took my hand and kissed it. "Talk to me. I know you're disappointed the way the evening turned out, but it wasn't all bad. Your mother and Bliss got along like gangbusters. I even had a good time. Bliss was open and friendly. You were right, she's not half as bad as I made her out to be."

"Yes. I'm glad you were impressed."

"Babe, tell me what's wrong. We just had a great time. Was I the only one? I could've sworn it was a good time had by all. I can't read your mind."

"Well that's odd. I could've swore you told me just the other morning that you can usually read people like a book. Guess you meant very shallow mind numbing books. The kind that bounce around with breast implants and ruby red lips looking for constant attention."

Jake shook his head as if he was in some type of vortex. "Okay. You got like ten seconds to tell me what you're talking about or this conversation is over," Jake said, suddenly tired of placating my anger. "Speak."

I bit my lip. I couldn't, I swore I wouldn't tell him about Bliss and her magic spell over my mother. I couldn't tell him how watching my mother and Bliss smile at each other made my stomach flip and dive to the point I could barely eat my food.

"Maybe I could talk to you if I wasn't afraid you were going to use everything I say against me later. I'm sick and tired of you telling me I'm crazy one minute, then agreeing with me the next. Why can't you just listen to me without judgment? Then I wouldn't be afraid to come to you."

He pulled me toward him to sit on his lap. He kissed my shoulder where my t-shirt had slipped off from the neckline stretching out over the years.

"Sirena showed up today at our lunch." I checked his face. He genuinely looked surprised.

"Why are you just now telling me this? So you've been stomping around mad at me all day because Sirena showed up?"

"Darcie put her up to it. She was already mic'd when she came in. It's some kind of game for Sirena. I swear, if she gets in my face one more time." I turned my face away so he wouldn't see the moisture budding in my eyes.

"I'll have a talk with Darcie. That kind of thing is not cool. I didn't know anything about it. You just got through lecturing me on secrets and then you're holding this inside all day."

"Jake, can I trust you to just listen. I don't need you to solve anything, just listen."

"I promise." He held up his hand of honor. "Talk to me," he said as if he had all the time in the world.

I began to tell him why I wanted Trevelle to meet Bliss, the real reason. I told him about Bliss touching my mother and suddenly making her the happiest woman on earth. Recounting everything to Jake sounded incredulous like a child rushing home from school to tell about the flying boy. *He put his arms out like this and he jumped from the sky and landed on his feet and then...*

With every breath I felt more and more like I'd imagined the entire afternoon, lucid, yet eternally floating.

"All I wanted was for Trevelle to spend some time around Bliss so she could read her vibe. I mean, I know Trevelle is a tad bit wacko, but she still has a real belief in the unseen. It's not all smoke, and mirrors. I wanted to see what she thought of Bliss and my mother. Maybe she could understand what was going on better than I could. Put it into simple terms."

"It's already in simple terms, babe. Bliss obviously has tapped into some kind of power through her own energy. It's natural to be afraid of someone like that. I felt it, saw exactly what you'd been telling me and it scared the shit out of me. Instead of coming up here and just outright saying that, I copped out and demanded she leave my house. But that was the cowardly approach. It had nothing to do with judging you or using what you already told me against you."

I let the relief escape my lungs. I curled up on his lap.

"But, umm, babe, your mother," he paused. "I kind of like her better this way. You think Bliss can keep her like this at least until she leaves."

I popped him on the shoulder. "Don't talk about my mama."

I put my head on his. "I like her this way too, but it's not real."

"It's real. The Oz never gave nothing to the Tin man he didn't already have. You know what that means? It means that person you're seeing, that side of your mother was already in there, probably wanting to come out."

"Oh yes, doctor, very good to know. I guess I should be grateful they're getting along doesn't matter how or why."

"That's right." Jake said before nibbling on the smooth skin on my shoulder. "I really think it's going to be okay. In a couple of weeks, Bliss will be on her way and everything will be back to normal."

"Wow, that must be why you get the big bucks, doctor."

"Yes, just call me Dr. Feelgood." He tried to slip his hand under my shirt. I clamped my arm shut so he couldn't reach his destination.

"I think this is taking advantage of the patient."

"You're officially cured. I'm no longer your doctor."

I turned my face away to avert his kiss. "Sorry, I think there's a twenty-four hour waiting period before there's any fraternizing with the patient."

I let him pull me backward against the soft duvet. More sexual content for the invisible tapes I imagined. Once again, if it was going to be viewed, might as well make it the best show possible.

A Bumpy Ride

"Good morning," my mother sang as she entered the kitchen. She'd dressed in a bright pink velour sweat suit. Her lips shimmered with bronze gloss. She came toward me for a kiss. Thank goodness it was only a cheek to cheek.

"Where'd you get that lip color? Something new?"

"Oh yes. Bliss and I stayed up talking late into the night. We exchanged a couple of colors."

The coffee I was drinking sputtered down my throat making me choke.

"Where are my grandchildren?" She asked before pouring herself a cup."

"They've already left for school. You're still on California time."

I had already been on my early morning walk. Bliss went with me and she hadn't mentioned a single thing about she and my mother's late night bonding party. Darcie sent the film crew to capture our walk and talk. Somehow it wasn't nearly as much fun knowing they were listening to every pant of my breath. I also couldn't ask or even hint about my mother's shift in personality. What was I going to say anyway? Ah, excuse me, sis, but did you put some kind of witch's spell on my mother.

"How'd you sleep, mom?"

"Ohhh, wonderful. My head hit the pillow and I didn't know who or where I was."

"Yeah, I was meaning to ask about that." Before I could finish my line of questioning, Bliss arrived.

"Hey there, Pauletta." She was freshly showered and wearing a navy blue sundress that nearly swallowed her thin frame. Her hands rested in the pockets, which meant she wasn't touching anyone for now.

I observed my mother. She beamed happiness and light. "Hey there, Bliss. What's on the agenda today? How about we head to the mall. Looks like Bliss could use some new clothes. And you too, Venus. Be my treat."

There was no doubt now. Pauletta Johnston was officially vexed. She offering to pay for a shopping trip to the mall was about as realistic as her and my dad skipping and holding hands.

"You all right, Venus?" My mom asked.

I lifted my head from where it was sunk into the palms of my confused hands. "Yeah, I'm fine."

"Well what do you think? Shopping. Just us girls?"

I faced Bliss and opened my mouth to a silent 'no'.

"Wouldn't miss it," she answered with a shrug to say she really didn't mind. Of course she didn't, it was probably her idea. Just like most of the thoughts my mother now had.

"We won't be joining you," Darcie's voice popped into the room, though there was no Darcie to be found. She was speaking from the two-way radio on the counter as if she was Bosley and we were Charlie's Angels. "We'll be filming

Jake the rest of the afternoon but we'll expect you back for dinner. Maybe you can plan an actual gathering we can film," she chided.

"You know, if the man didn't want to be filmed, that's his right," I shot back.

"Relax, sweetie. Yelling at the hand that feeds you is not a good idea," my mother advised.

I rolled my eyes at the same time. "I can't wait until this filming season is over."

"I love it. I think it's fun."

"Mom, it's not going to be fun when you see yourself on television six months from now and wish you could've said and did every single thing differently."

"Life is for living in the here and now. Why would I want to do anything differently?"

"Mom, you basically gave permission to the production company to do whatever the hell they liked with your face, body, and soul. Did you bother to read that disclosure before you signed it?"

Darcie spoke up again. "It simply gives us permission to include you in the entire show, Mrs. Johnston. We're so honored to have you in the show. You can tell all your friends to watch."

"The joys of fame." I worked my way off the breakfast stool. The smoothie Jake left me to drink only made me hungrier and cranky.

"Apparently, something you've grown tired of," Darcie snapped over the intercom.

"What's with the attitude?"

What's with yours? I wanted to ask my mother in return. In the meantime I picked up the radio and tossed it into the freezer and slammed the door shut.

"I'm going to go get ready for our shopping trip," Bliss announced.

"What changed your mind?" I asked my mother once Bliss was out of sight. "You come here ready to tear everybody a new one and suddenly you're Miss Congeniality."

"I don't know. I guess I just feel free of stress and anxiety. Bliss is such a nice young lady. You know what she told me last night, anyone that's stuck holding a grudge has no future to look towards. And I agree. Life is too short. I want to move forward, not be stuck in the past."

"I'm glad you like her. I really like her too. It's just that I wanted you to like her on your own. I wanted you to get to know her and see for yourself."

"Oh I did. You didn't force me at all. You know, it feels good. I can honestly say, I have nothing bad on my mind."

"That's good, mom. We should all be so lucky."

I heard the doorbell as I was headed up the stairs. I did an about face and headed down before Darcie sent the cameraman. Through the peephole all I saw was a huge floral arrangement being held with a hand full of rings on each finger wrapped around the vase.

"Special delivery," Trevelle announced.

"What took you so long?"

"Why, whatever do you mean? Am I late? You know God may not come when you call but he's always on time." Trevelle said fully rehearsed.

"There's no one filming right now, sorry."

"But you said all day."

"I know, but they're in Jake's studio now. He's working in there." I tried to take the arrangement from her hands.

"I might as well take this back to the shop. You've already had your weekly delivery."

I yanked it from her long cold fingers. "Give me my flowers and get in here," I said determined to restore order in my house.

Trevelle took a few steps past the foyer and stopped abruptly. "Whoa." She put up her hands. "Hold on. There's something going on here."

I turned around to see, Bobby, the cameraman locked and loaded. I should've known.

"There's a presence in this house," Trevelle said.

"Really? You're not just saying that for the camera?" I hung on her next words.

"I'm telling you..." She squeezed her eyes shut. "There it is again. Did you feel that?" She wrapped her arms around herself and shivered from the imaginary cold.

"No. I didn't feel anything. Trevelle, are you serious?" I whispered. "Are you doing this for effect or do you really feel something?" It was exactly what I'd expected, but I still wasn't sure if Trevelle was putting on an act. After the evening's disappointment with her not getting her chance in front of the camera, it sort of tainted the results of the findings.

"Oh yes, this is real. A lot of negative energy is stored in this house. We've got to have an immediate intervention.

Holy water. Prayer. Time to exorcise the negative spirit. I can't believe..." She began to shake her hands and hum. "Cast this demon out, Lord."

"Trevelle, does the spirit have a name?"

"It's a woman full of anger and vengeance and it's directed at you." She grabbed her head covering her ears. "This is too much. I'm not prepared for this."

"Prepared how? I can get you a Bible. Is that what you need?"

"My own spirit has been drained these last few days. I just don't have the reserves for this kind of thing."

"Trevelle, please don't go. Stay."

She was already out the door, clicking her heels down the pathway to the In Bloom van. She wasted no time starting the engine and nearly backing into the circular fountain before shifting the gear into drive and peeling off.

I turned slowly to see the camera still aiming in my direction. Trevelle wasn't the type to ever run from a chance to be on television. That was reason enough to know she wasn't making anything up. So great, now the world would know my house was possessed, or at least my mother was. My dear sweet sister was the source, I was sure of it. Could I still take her under my wing if she was some kind of demon seed? The thought sent chills all over my body. Now it was me standing rubbing the cold off my arms.

Darcie appeared from where she'd probably been watching the entire scene on her digital feed. "Are you all right? Should I call someone?"

"I'm fine."

"Are you sure? You don't look good."

"What are you doing here? I thought you were filming Jake in the studio? All of a sudden I look up and I'm being taped. We really have to stop meeting like this, Bobby."

He grinned and forced himself to stop. No fraternizing with the show clowns, which was exactly how I felt. Like I was the bearded lady on display. I sat down on the base of the stairs, grabbing the banister to keep my balance.

"I said we'd be filming in your husband's studio later today, therefore we couldn't follow you shopping." She smiled. "Shelly, get Venus some water, please. Fast."

It was true. I didn't feel well. The lightheadedness came and went without any warning. I examined myself with my hand to my forehead. Maybe I was running a fever. Nope. Cool as a cucumber.

Shelly showed up with a bottle of Evian. "Here you go, Venus."

"Thank you." I took a swig.

Darcie sat down next to me. I should've known what was coming next.

"You know, I think that would be pretty exciting to have some kind of séance. Can you imagine the interest in something like that? That friend of yours, is she authentic? You know what, doesn't matter. We can find a psychic. Someone who talks to the dead."

"What if the one who needs talking to is very much alive?" I sighed then found the strength to get up and walk away without a word.

Picture Worth A Thousand Words

Sirena opened her compact and gave her cheeks a soft pat of bronzer. She stared at herself in the mirror, grateful to have her glow back. Maybe it was the cheap drug store make-up she had to buy or maybe it was being in the same room with Jay. She could feel the energy running through her body.

She peeked both ways before coming out of the powder room. Venus would have a hissy fit if they bumped into each other in her own hallway. But where else was she supposed to go tinkle? Jay had designed his home studio in the back of the house but had forgotten one important thing in the plans. A bathroom. He'd warned her not to take one step beyond it and to come right back. She didn't want to piss him off so she'd made sure the coast was clear.

Now there were voices coming from down the hall. Sirena heard very little of exactly what was said, only that someone was panicked, shrieking about holy water and demons.

Figured. Some Jehovah Witness had probably stopped by and made out like a bandit. The gullible Venus would fall for anything.

After it got quiet, she tiptoed out the way same way she'd come in. It was too early in the game to have Venus running to Jay, making her demands to end their working relationship. She had to at least look as if she was playing by the rules. Stay out of her sight, he'd warned. Do not come within a hundred feet of her. He was so angry after he'd found out about her crashing the little tea party at Briar Patch, as if Venus owned the entire restaurant.

She made sure her white blouse was unbuttoned to the lowest point of decency, and tucked into her jeans properly to show her tiny waist and flat stomach. It made her look conservative, yet sexy as hell. She knew Jay's taste. He liked the simple clean look but with a dash of spice. Having to look at his frumpy wife for the past few months only made him easier for the pickings. But she wasn't trying to just sleep with him, not this time. She wanted the entire package. She'd even had the nerve to shop for rings, it didn't hurt to look and be fully prepared. She didn't want to be one of those wishy washy dames who didn't know what she wanted and dragged her man around from store to store to look at the same cut diamonds all over town.

When she arrived back in the studio, he was leaning back in his chair.

She squeezed into the seat next to him and turned on her pearly whites for the cameraman who'd just arrived. "So let's hear what you got."

Jay handed her the headphones and she pushed them away.

"Nah, I want to hear this thing popping. Nice and loud."

"All right. But don't be mad at me when you hear a bootleg copy go viral before it even gets out the gate." Jay cranked it up. The beat was fierce. She bounced and jiggled in her seat. Her voice flowed for a few seconds and then Jay's authenticity kicked in. His rap was so smooth and honest. There were few artists left who had a genuine lyrical sound. He closed his eyes and smiled when the song was fading out.

Sirena had to contain herself. She wanted to stroke his smooth face and plant a kiss so deep on his lips he'd lose his faculties. She raised her arms and slapped him high five instead of the kiss. "You rock. I swear, nobody's got it like you."

"I think we did it. This is your hit right here." He was proud and happier than she'd seen him in a long time.

She wanted nothing more than to save him from his miserable life.

"You mean our hit. We've always been a good team." She had to reign in her emotions. Any moment and she could burst into begging mode. "So what do we do next?" As if she didn't know. But she couldn't let on that she could take it from here. No. His services were long from being over.

"Get a meeting with your people at Delong Records. This thing is gold. Their going to want to back a huge album release with this one."

"I know, right. But these record companies are scared of failing on an epic level. You gotta come with me, Jay. Pitch it the only way it can be pitched. Come to New York and sit down with them. Show them that you're willing to back me up. Maybe even go on tour with me. That way they know it will sell. They'll get the guarantee they need to make this thing happen."

The pressure seemed to take the air out of the room. She knew he was torn.

"CiCi, I agreed to produce one song. One beat. I'm not trying to do an entire set. That's not going to fly."

"You mean it's not going to fly with wifey?" She held her tongue to say more. She remembered the camera. All she had to do was push a bit harder. "Please, Jay. Like you said, this record is gold, hey maybe even platinum," she played with the words and dangled them like carrots. "But we won't know if it doesn't get the full push. You know how these things work. If the record company isn't behind you, no matter how good it is, you know what happens. It'll never see the light of day."

"Yeah. I know, but..." he spun his chair around and picked up his cell phone. "Yeah, babe. Yeah. Okay. Give me ten minutes I'll be right there." Jay turned his attention back to the music board. He flipped a couple of switches and powered down.

"I know you're a dedicated father and husband. You are truly the perfect family guy, but the babies have to eat, right" She turned her smile to full wattage. "Somebody's gotta fund this operation," she said trying to keep it light. She could warn him, one day you have it all and the next, you're about to lose your house. It could happen to anyone. But not if they worked together, stuck together, she wanted to say out loud. Everyone disappeared when the well ran dry, but they could survive anything together.

"Let me give it some thought. All right. I'm not promising anything." He stood up. "I'll call you, let you know my decision."

She ignored his neutral answer. "Don't you want to see your name back on the Billboard chart? I know you got a couple of endorsements rolling your way. But Jay, come on, I know you miss the high of being on top of the chart. This is the record."

Jay finally cracked. "Yeah, set up the meeting. I'll see what I can do."

Sirena left their circus palace over the moon. She had not been this thrilled in some time.

Baby steps, she kept telling herself. It was all coming together. Her plan couldn't have been more perfect.

All except one loose end. Venus was still in the way. She'd gone through her assassin's wallet when he fell asleep in her bed. His real name was Lucas Heights. She didn't bother telling him that she had gone through his wallet and pockets, or that she'd taken a thousand of the money out of the envelope she had given him of her own money.

He seemed to only be satisfied that he got what he'd come for. Good to know her ass was still worth something, contrary to how the industry had made her feel.

When, she'd asked. When was it going to happen? She needed some kind of date, time, and guarantee. But soon, was all he answered. She had a feeling he'd be back again for one more payment. She couldn't say she'd refuse. He was good in bed. Good in the hallway, the shower, kitchen, and on the floor. The man knew how to get to the point. Too bad she could never have real feelings for him. But it didn't stop her from heating up every time she remembered the forceful way he handled his business.

She peeked at herself in the rearview mirror of her car. Her eyes were bright and filled with possibility. She wished she could take a picture of herself this happy so she could remember how good it felt.

A hit record, the man of her dreams, all within reach if Lucas just did what she'd paid him for. What she was continually paying him for.

The Problem With Venus

When people first met me, they assumed I had some sort of mystical nature. The funky wild untamed hair meant I didn't play by the rules. I was a free spirit who accepted all and judged no one. I got it everywhere I went, the sly smile, wink, or understanding nod from a fellow unique soul who understood the journey of being one with the universe.

Natural hair signified freedom of rules. True. But it also signified a convenient way of life. I'd given up chemically straightening my hair years earlier out of protest. Refusing to give my hard earned money and two Saturdays a month to keeping it straight and shiny. Sometimes the smell of singed hair still crept up my nostrils like a bad dream. But it didn't mean I had lost my mind or didn't know the rules of life. I knew up and I knew down. I'd always slapped myself on the back for being smarter than the average bear. Yet, people continually took me for granted, thinking I'd accept any wooden nickel and sing Ole Happy Day on demand.

I wasn't happy and I wasn't about to sit around and let Bliss make a fool of me another minute longer. I'd trusted her, put her before my own good sense, and ignored all the red flags because I wanted a sister more than I wanted to believe she was some kind of anti-Christ.

I watched from the window as the car I'd hired pulled out of the driveway with my mother and Bliss in tow. I waited for Jake to come inside the house after I'd called and told him I was going on a reconnaissance mission. He came inside and I immediately swept him up the stairs. I quickly filled him in on Trevelle's visit and running out the door like her hair was on fire.

"Her hair caught fire?"

"Honey, no. Not literally. I just meant she felt some kind of demon and couldn't take a second more in our house."

"Well why didn't she feel that way last night?"

"That's what I asked, but apparently she wasn't open to receive the energy."

"Yeah, too busy trying to get on camera."

"Come on, Bliss and my mom went to the mall. We've got free reign to check things out."

"You sure you want to do this?" Jake had always warned me, if you seek-you-shall-find. Therefore, if you don't want to know, stop looking. I couldn't stop myself. I turned the doorknob and stuck my face into the guestroom where Bliss was staying.

"All clear."

Jake followed me inside. It smelled like her. Always that light peachiness floating in the air. Jake went for the closet. I started with her drawers. Sparse. T-shirts, bra, sleep gowns, a ball of hair in a plastic baggy.

I went to the next drawer but a few seconds later the question, who's hair was in the plastic baggy, begged to be answered. Especially since it looked exactly like the same puffball I'd thrown away after my last wash and comb out. No one else had my hair in the Johnston-Parson household.

I pulled it out and inspected it with a sniff.

"Babe, come quick."

Jake came into the room. I held it up. "Look at this."

"Hair?"

"Yes. Sniff?" I ordered.

He curled up his nose, prepared for the worse. His face relaxed in a pleasant surprise. It was the unmistakable scent of my hair. Probably his favorite scent.

"Now that's just freaky," Jake said bewildered when normally he had an answer for everything. Not this time. We both had question marks over our foreheads. My hands started to shake as I went through the next set of drawers. I was afraid of what else I'd find.

I went into the closet and kneeled down to unzip her suitcase. I lifted it open slowly and sighed with relief when it was empty. Glad there was nothing else as creepy as the plastic bag of hair.

Jake stood over me as I checked the side compartment. I reached in and came out with a wad of folded cash, all crisp new one hundred dollar bills. My hands continued to shake as I pushed the money back into the compartment where I found it.

I checked all the other zipped spaces, nothing. Before I closed the suitcase back I heard buzzing. I placed my hands on the edges. "Did you hear that? It's definitely a phone."

Jake helped me flip the suitcase over. There were no other compartments. Where then? The sound stopped, but I continued my search. At the bottom of the suitcase between the wheels was a clever compartment. Not even a professional snooper could've guessed to look there. I was sort of proud of spy capabilities. I pulled back the Velcro and then a second layer with a zipper and there it was, a phone nestled in the dark space.

I mean, really? Was it that serious? She could've kept the phone in her purse like a normal person. No one would've cared or bothered to investigate her callers. Now that it was hidden like Fort Knox all that mattered was finding out who, what, and why. I flipped open the tiny phone. The missed call read, Mom. Either "Mom" was sending messages from the grave or she was alive somewhere sipping on iced-tea and Bliss had lied about her mother dying.

I stood up, maybe too quickly. The room spun. I had a firm grip on the door handle and Jake trying to get my bearings.

"What's going on? You all right?" Jake kept me balanced. "Come on, I knew this wasn't a good idea. Let's get out of here. We've seen enough."

"No. I want to hear this." I still held the phone tightly against my hip. There was too much information to digest but still not enough. With my head swirling I assessed the situation. A bag of my hair. A hidden phone. An envelope full of money. A voice message. There was no turning back. I pushed the button and listened.

I put the phone between Jake and I so he could hear it too. We heard everything loud and clear. There was nothing left to do. I hunched my shoulders. "She lied. Her mother is obviously alive and well. This message proves it. She asked if she'd done what she was asked to do? What do you think that is?" I stared up at Jake with sad eyes.

I closed the phone and shoved it back in the suitcase. Jake helped me scoot everything back where we'd found it.

As my mother and Bliss pulled up, I was prepping myself for the inquiry. I would've made a great lawyer. If only I could've stomached four more years of college on top of the five I'd endured.

I headed downstairs to greet my sister.

"Hey, where are you?" Bliss called out.

I heard the rattle of shopping bags and hoped my mother kept the receipts.

"Did you two have a good time?" I folded my arms across my chest to let Bliss know she had some explaining to do.

"It would've been more fun if you'd come," she answered, pretending not to know full well there was trouble ahead.

"Bliss, I need to speak with you." I realized Darcie was on the scene and the tape was rolling, but I wasn't concerned with anyone except my dear sweet sister.

"I'm famished. Can it wait until we've had these delicious cupcakes?" She introduced them as if she'd baked them herself. "Come on, try one."

"No. I can't."

"Oh, try one." Pauletta sang. "They're the size of a thimble. Not going to hurt one bit."

"Mom, I really need to talk to Bliss, alone. Do you mind going to check on the twins?" She peered between Bliss and I. Only after Bliss said it was okay, did she take off.

A few seconds later, Jake appeared. He came inside as if it was an accidental visit. "Hey there, sweetheart. How's it going?" He planted a kiss on my lips then leaned against the counter ready to watch the fireworks. "How was your shopping trip, Bliss?"

"Nice," Bliss said curtly, hardly falling for the accidental drop in. She knew she was being double-teamed. Two against one. Not that it was necessary. I wasn't afraid of Bliss, at least not anymore. She was just a regular old human being who lied like the rest of us. And if she wanted to hurt me, she could've done it already. But this was the worst possible way, making me believe and trust her only to have it all thrown in my face.

"Babe, if you're finished for the day, do you mind picking up Mya and Christopher from school? Ursula has the rest of the day off."

"No problem." Jake took a peek at his phone but didn't move. "I have a few minutes," he said, anticipating the answers we both wanted.

"No, really, it's okay to get there early." I forced the issue and tried not to grit my teeth. "Please. If you don't mind."

"Right. Okay." He was disappointed. But he was going to have to wait. Though the cameraman and about three other people were in the room, I still needed to have the one-on-one attention between me and Bliss.

She sat down and took a small bite out of her creamy cupcake. I sat down too. "Are you sure you don't want one? You don't know what you're missing."

"I found your stash of cash and your secret phone," I said, getting it off my chest. "You want to tell me why you lied about your mother, why you said she passed away when she's very much alive."

"You want to have this conversation here?" Her arms were now folded over her chest.

"Hey, I'm not the one with something to hide."

"We all have something to hide." Bliss said as if giving me fair warning.

"But I'm not the one with a bag full of your hair hidden in a drawer either. Yeah, ahuh, found that too. Nope. I can honestly say I'm an open book."

"You went through my things. How very sisterly of you?" She pushed her wavy hair behind her ear and took the last bite of her cupcake. "For your information, I took the hair after your mother made a very valid point. What if we forged ahead with our new relationship only to find out we weren't related after all? I wasn't sure if it would work, but I was going to use it for a DNA sibling test. I'd read about it, but then I decided, not to let that kind of doubt get in the way. I liked you as my sister, my friend, and would trust what I know to be true. You and I are sisters. So ask me what you are dying to ask? Say whatever's on your mind."

"I heard the message from your mother." My voice squeaked feeling a wave of guilt for having listened in the first place. Somehow she'd managed to turn the tables on me. Here she was the one who'd been found out and all her deception and she easily made me feel like I'd betrayed her.

I tried to shake off the blame and forge ahead with my questions. "I thought she died. So did you make all of this up? I believed you. Now I know what's really going on."

Her lips turned up into a smile. She took a deep breath and leaned toward me. "You have no idea."

"Then tell me. Explain," I screamed. "Stop playing games and tell me what the hell is going on."

"You basically want me to make you feel better about snooping through my things. When you're the one who should be ashamed of yourself."

"I am not ashamed. This is my house. You were invited here and I trusted you."

She put her hand out and stroked my arm. "You can trust me," she said. I braced myself for some kind of mind meld. I squeezed my eyes closed and waited for the transformation. I opened them back up one at a time. At first I felt nothing.

But within seconds, my tone changed. I could hear myself speaking but there was another side of me disagreeing with everything coming out of my mouth. *You expect me to believe that?* "I guess you're right. I'm sorry for doubting you. You've been nothing but honest and kind." *Get out of my house. Leave and don't come back.* I wanted to tell her I would believe nothing she was about to say. She could talk all day and into the night and she'd be wasting her time. But instead I sat patiently with my head slightly tilted waiting for whatever she wanted to tell me and I was sure it would all make sense.

"That's true. I've been nothing but honest and kind. The minute I came to your house, I felt this bond. I'd never lie to you, you have to know that."

I nodded my head like a small child. I listened with eyes and ears, fully accepting.

Bliss leaned in close. Peaches. "Ask me anything you want to know."

"Are you my father's child?"

"As far as I know, yes. That's what I was told but since I've never spent a minute of my life with him, I guess one could argue differently."

"Why did you lie about your mother? She called and left you a message. I heard the message."

"My mother passed away when I was five years old. So yes, I bent the truth slightly. The person that you heard was my grandmother. I call her Mom. I always have."

"But you said you had no one. Even your grandmother had passed away."

"That was the grandmother on my mother's side. This is my grandmother from my father's side. And yours too. Her name is Sarah."

It took a minute to gather what she'd just said. "Sarah Johnston. No. My Grandma Sadie? My grandmother died a long time ago. I think you're mistaken."

Bliss pressed a kiss on my forehead. "She loves you. She always has."

It was all too much. My head was ringing with criss crossed messages. I tried to stop the talking in my head. The dual frequencies of wanting to believe Bliss but knowing she was the enemy. But she smelled like peaches. Bad people didn't smell like springtime, did they?

When I looked up, Pauletta was standing in the kitchen with a hard glare in her eyes. I popped off the chair, perky and filled with more energy than I'd had in a long time. "Mom, did you hear what she said about Grandma Sadie? You told me she had gotten sick and I thought she'd died. But good news, she's fine. Bliss has spent time with her. Isn't this wonderful?" I smiled with glee but the dual messenger in my head saw the scowl on my mother's face and quickly understood it was hardly wonderful. More like the worst news ever.

"Well isn't this special," Pauletta said, which may have gone down as her shortest response to a question ever. She stood with her arms folded over her chest.

"She actually raised me," Bliss spoke up. "My mother wasn't able to take care of me. I was in a foster home for three months before she found me. She had pictures of Venus all over the house. I used to stare at them and constantly ask when I was going to meet this perfect sister that I admired, and she didn't know I existed." Bliss had tears in her eyes. However she was still smiling. I knew that feeling. I understood it perfectly well.

"It's okay," I mumbled. "I'm here now. But I'm far from perfect." I was about to reach over and hug Bliss when I felt my mother's hand squeeze around my neck.

"Do not trust her." My mother's tone was harsh. Her lips curled up in a snarl. Apparently the spell was only good for one customer at a time. I was light as air but my mother had come down hard. "That woman, your grandma Sadie," she spat, "never spoke a kind word to me and she welcomed you, her son's whore child?"

"I should probably leave," Bliss announced. "I just want you to know that she loves you," Bliss said to me before rising from the dining table.

"You're right about that. You should leave," Pauletta shouted. "And don't ever come back."

"Mom, what're you doing? Stop it."

"That little heifer has been conspiring with your Grandma Sadie. What else do you need to know? Get her out of this house."

"What? No," I shook my head trying to control all the incoming messages. Bliss was the enemy. My mother lied. My father lied. Love everyone. Trust no one. I pressed my fingers to my temples. "Listen to me," I said feeling the room begin to spin.

"I'm not listening for anything except the door to close on her way out."

I felt Bliss behind me. "You should sit down." She touched me with both hands and led me back to the dining room chair. Within seconds I was back to being clear headed.

"Mom, this is my house. It's up to me whether Bliss stays or goes."

"That woman treated me like I was gum on the bottom of her shoe. I was never good enough. I heard her myself tell your father I would never do right by him and I wasn't going to do nothing but make him miserable. Nothing about me was good enough for that woman. Do you understand what I'm telling you? And then she takes in his bastard child. You're damn right I told you she was gone and buried. I was never going to let you see that woman again. Not unless it was over my dead body."

It was like a movie reel began to play in my head. *That woman* was my grandmother, Sarah Johnston of Little Rock, Arkansas who'd raised my father all by herself cleaning houses until the day one of her employers left her a hefty sum in her Will right along with ten acres of land. She had to be 80-something now, maybe close to 90, and probably still wearing her shiny hair pulled back in a bun.

There seemed to be a rivalry between the two women no one could put to rest. My mother believed she was doing Henry Johnston a favor by choosing him but Sarah Johnston believed the exact opposite. It was Pauletta who would never be good enough for her son and she wasn't shy about making her opinion known.

I'd heard about their inability to be in the same room, which explained why Timothy and I only got to visit with her a few times when we were small. I loved being in her house, the smell of beans always simmering on the stove. Morning breakfasts with a full spread of crispy bacon, cheesy grits, and buttered pancakes. There'd be a long white platter covered with big juicy slices of tomatoes and watermelon from her garden and right next to it a plate of hot steaming grits.

When my father visited he had to go alone. He'd pack his suitcase by himself unlike when he traveled on business and my mother would lay everything out for him a day or two earlier. Only after Timothy was about ten and I seven or eight years old, did she let us go with him. The hot drive in the car would take two whole days, but it was worth the long road trip to spend time alone with our father. We would play our music loud with the windows down, stop at drive-through burger joints, and order the greasiest, saltiest, delicious fast food I'd ever tasted. All the things Pauletta would never have allowed.

The last time I remembered my father announcing one of his trips, I did my usual happy dance and was headed off to start packing my Disney Cinderella suitcase when my mother erupted and said very clearly, "not this time. You see, she is very ill, so your father has to go alone. It's very sad. She doesn't want you and Timothy to see her this way."

I cried my eyes out. I eventually believed Grandma Sadie had died because no matter how many times I brought up her name my mother would only avert the conversation. I thought she was protecting me. I never knew anyone who'd died. Looking back, I could see my father's face tight with grief that was probably anger from my mother's lie.

"That woman hated me." Pauletta pointed her finger at Bliss. "She went and found you just to spite me, just to throw this whole ugly mess in my face."

"That's between you and her. I had nothing to do with that," Bliss said gently though the power her voice lent made me afraid of what could possibly happen next.

"Mom, please, stop," I said out of fear.

"I won't stand for your betrayal too. You decide, either she leaves or I do."

Bliss cut her eyes toward me. I didn't know what to say but she seemed to understand that my mother meant the world to me. Whatever she may have thought about doing or saying, she decided to back down.

"I'll go. You don't have to make that choice. Just remember that I am on your side," she said to me. She faced Pauletta. "You want me to tell you about my grandmother." Bliss blinked away the budding moisture. "She's a kind and sweet woman who tried to make up for the fact that her son couldn't stand up and be a man. So you're right, maybe you were too good for him. Maybe we all are."

I took a hold of my mother's hand. It was a harsh blow. Bliss had spoken the truth and it left chills running down my arms. What she said had rightly summed up the entire situation. And it hurt. None of us would be standing there pitted against one another if not for his actions or inaction as the case seemed to be.

After The Storm

After Bliss left and my mother retreated to her room, I closed myself off in the nursery, probably the only place in the house I felt safe.

How I got myself into these situations was never clear. No matter how I replayed each step, I still ended up standing in the middle of quicksand. Regardless of which direction, or choice, they all seemed to lead to the same place where I sank deeper into the wet gooey mess. How is it I never came out clean in the end? Everything was my fault. It boggled the mind. But not in the room with Lauren and Henry, there I could do no wrong.

I held Lauren by her hands and let her chubby legs bounce while she tried to stand. Her smiling and slobbering with joy made me forget momentarily the chaos of the day. She has no idea her mommy is a troublemaker. Had I not gone snooping into Bliss's luggage, I would've never found the phone, never discussed it in front of my mom, and never found out about Bliss and Sadie's relationship.

For whatever value it held, I was sorry.

I kissed Lauren on the nose. But it's Henry who squealed with delight as if he felt the kiss from the other side of the room. "Let's go see what brother is so happy about." I rose up with Lauren and went to the crib. "Look who's awake."

He was doing his best to pull himself up and stand against the crib railing. He reached his hand out to me and I gave him a pull up. I leaned over and kissed him between his big brown eyes. Lauren batted at my chin wanting my full attention.

I already felt the entanglement of being in the middle. Why did we have to choose loyalties? Families should be exempt from choosing sides. I prayed when Lauren and Henry grew up they would never have any battles. Brothers and sisters, mothers and fathers, we were supposed to know better. But then again, we're only human.

"I knew I'd find you in here." Jake came inside. With the sound of his voice, Henry got even more excited. Jake came over and lifted him easily into his strong arms.

"Well, you warned me. You told me it was a bad idea to go snooping and now Bliss is gone and my mom is packing as we speak. Man, it was crazy."

"At this point there's not much else that can surprise me," Jake said with his lips against Henry's full head of curls.

I told him everything he missed. I left out the parts that were sketchy. Unable to explain how I felt trapped in my own head. The way I felt one way but said the other. "If you want a play by play, I'm sure Darcie would be happy to show you the tape. I think we met our quota for drama."

"How'd you leave it with Bliss?"

"She probably never wants to see me again. And my mother...I just don't know. She lied to me about my grandmother. I don't know whether to feel sorry for her or be mad."

"Wow, this is some major Peyton Place kind of stuff."

"I want Bliss in my life. I don't want to have to choose between my mother and all the past in between. It's my decision and no one else's," I said, grateful to have my own mind back.

Right Back At ya

Sirena awakened to the sound of birds chirping outside her window. Birds were disgusting and filthy. She hated the thought of them perched on her deck doing their business and expecting her to clean it up. She tried to go back to sleep and dream about her future that was beginning to finally look bright. Things were coming together. The record she and Jay put down was going to be a hit. Step one. Showing him she could be a good friend would be Step two. Helping him with the loss of his wife would be Step three. If only she could get to Step three.

Her knight in assassin armor had promised it was going to happen any day now. Soon, he'd whispered in her ear after she'd slept with him for the fourth time. If sleeping together was what she could call it. He'd pulled her hair and damn near strangled her once. She never thought she'd be the type that liked it rough. She pushed herself deeper into the mattress thinking of what he'd do to her next.

Squawk!

"Good grief." She popped up from bed and went to the window. She threw the curtain back. A large crow screeched before taking off. Disgusting black and white speckled piles decorated the corner where they'd made their quarters. She shouldn't care. Not like it was going to be her home that much longer. But for now, she needed some damn peace.

She slapped on the window. "Go. Beat it," she threatened. Wings fluttered and took flight. But there was one that refused to go. It stayed, standing firm on the banister of the deck. "Beat it. Swoosh, go," she yelled and waved her arms. It merely looked in the other direction unafraid.

She left and came back with a broom. She swung it back and forth but far enough not to actually hit it. Still the crow remained unfettered.

"That's it. Your ass is going down." Sirena took a step forward and jabbed the broom toward the crow. It flew up, dodging her blow and landed a couple of feet away. She swung again, it dodged again. Before long, Sirena was in a full out sweat. She didn't know how long she'd been fighting with the bird, but realized it was winning.

"Okay. I know what you need." She went back inside. She peeked out the curtain, still not believing it's determination not to leave. When she came back with her surprise weapon, there were ten or more crows in line. She looked at the pepper spray in her palm, and hesitated. Would it be enough?

"Get off my property," she huffed before pushing the spray forward. They screeched before flying away. All but one. The crow with hard beady eyes continued to face her. The black shiny wings expanded and headed directly toward Sirena. She screamed before raising the pepper spray. Liquid streamed high in the air but the force of the crow's wings sent the spray back into her face.

Up and away, the crow kept going, soaring, and she'd felt victorious until she felt the stinging pain. First it was her eyes burning. Then her nose, lips and ears felt like they were on fire. She gasped to cry out but her throat began to burn too. She rushed into the house, straight to the bathroom and stuck her face under the cool faucet sucking down as much water as she could get. The heat intensified.

She got into the shower and took relief in the cold water pouring over her head. As much as she wanted to cry, she held it together. She couldn't let a flock of birds ruin her day. She had too much to look forward to. She had to pack for her trip to New York with Jay. They were scheduled to meet with the executives of the record company tomorrow. This was her chance to get back on top. The music was on point and everything she'd dreamt was coming to fruition. No stupid birds were going to stop her from what she was due.

The towel was within reach but her vision was blurred from the pepper spray. She grabbed it and patted gently before slightly opening her eyes. The towel seemed to have started the burning all over again. She went to the mirror and squinted at her reflection. Red puffy blotches were everywhere. She looked like she'd been beaten up. Please. No. She leaned in closer for better inspection. Maybe it was only swelling and not third degree burns as they appeared. Either way, she didn't know how her face would be clear by the time she met with the record execs.

Behind her in the mirror something moved. She twisted around. She screamed when she saw the black crow standing on the edge of the bathtub, cocky as ever. "Get out," she cried at the top of her lungs before reaching for a can of mousse and hurling it.

She missed by a long shot and happened to barely miss Lucas when he appeared through her bathroom door.

"What's going on? I heard you screaming all the way from outside when I pulled up."

"Look at me. Look at my face. That thing is trying to kill me. My face won't stop burning." The bird stood proud moving it's head from him to her.

He put out his hand. "Come here."

She took his hand. He pulled her close before pushing her behind him. He reached under his jacket and took out the gun he kept holstered against his chest.

"You're going to shoot it?"

"What do you want me to do?"

"You see my face. That's the result of me trying to aim pepper spray. The same way you'll probably end up shooting yourself. It's something crazy about it. I'm telling you. I just want to get out of here. Please, I think I may have to go to the hospital. Look at my face," she waited, still, determined not to cry. Salty tears would only make her face more ablaze.

They scooted out without turning their back to the dangerous bird. He slammed the door shut. "Maybe it'll starve to death. You don't have anything it can eat in there do you?"

"Not unless it likes make-up, soap and a lot of lotion." She shook her hands off to the side. "I'm dying here."

"I know what to do." Again, he took her hand. She hadn't expected him to be so gentle. Not the way he treated her in bed. Downstairs, in the kitchen he poured a bowl of milk. He used a clean towel, dabbing it first in the milk, then on her red welts.

The relief was almost instant. She reached for the carton with the intent of pouring the entire thing over her face. It was empty. She directed her gaze to the bowl.

"Hold on, kitty cat. Trust me, this is the best way," he said guarding the bowl.

"Well, hurry up. Can't you move faster?"

"Why am I not surprised? Miss Got to Be In Control." He blotted the corners of her mouth then kissed her on the lips. "Where else does it hurt?"

She exhaled liberation. Free at last from the excruciating pain. "I think I can take it from here."

"Just relax. I got you."

How many times in her life had she heard that? "Really? You got me, huh? Then why is that bitch still walking around?"

"Didn't your mother teach you not to bite the hand that feeds you? Or the one soothing your pain?"

"My mother left me and my father when I was eight years old. She taught me one thing. If it ain't right, make a change. Do what you have to do?"

"Oh, so you're a tough chick, huh? So tough, you pining over some brotha who don't even want you?"

"Just do what I paid you to do." She snatched the towel from his hand. She dunked it into the milk until every ounce was soaked and rested it over her face, covering her nose and eyes like a mummy.

When she pulled the towel away, he was gone. She was alone sitting on the breakfast nook stool. The house was silent. For the first time in her life she was frightened of being alone.

Wrestling With Fate

"CiCi, something's come up," Jay said into the phone. "I'm not going to make it to New York with you."

Sirena was already driving to the airport. She'd called to make sure Jay was doing the same. She turned the music down in her car to be sure she'd heard him correctly. "What? No, Jay. You have to go with me. You know how hard it was setting up this meeting, I can't reschedule."

"There's a lot going on in the household. I can't leave right now. Listen, you'll do fine. The work speaks for itself. Just drop the CD in the player and watch them smile."

"I can't believe you're letting me down like this. I can't believe it. Oh wait, yes I can. It's probably Venus and her issues, right. Another crisis. When you gonna stop babysitting, and I'm not talking about your kids. I'm talking about her."

"I'm going to stop you right there. I've asked you to keep my wife's name out of your mouth. I can't play this game with you anymore. The disrespect has got to stop."

"Or what?" She screamed. "Or what? What else could you do to me? You've already let me be destroyed by the media. My career was ruined because you let everyone believe I was a lying wench. What else could you do to me that hasn't already been done?"

He was silent for a few seconds too long. Probably thinking she absolutely was a lying wench, but who made him the judge and jury? Dead air made her think he'd hung up. "I'm sorry, Jay. Okay. Are you there?"

"I'm here," he said letting his frustration escape in the tone of his voice.

"I'm just so upset," Sirena whispered doing her best to sound as pitiful as possible. "I didn't mean what I said. I'm desperate. I need this. You can be up to New York and back before dinner. Please," she begged. "You won't even have to tell dear wifey. I can keep a secret."

"No arguing with you there." He sounded like he was outside. Probably making his phone call away from anyone who might hear him. "I can't go. That's all there is to it," he said sounding more resolute by the minute.

This wasn't happening. She pulled the car over and flicked on the hazard lights. Cars sped by every few seconds leaving her a nervous wreck. "Jake, please, I need this. You of all people know what this means to me. We've always been there for each other. Why should anything change now?"

"I can't keep trying to make you understand. I said I'd back you up on this record. Hell, I wrote and produced the thing knowing full well it would cause problems in my household. But right now, my family comes first. I'm sorry if that hurts you. Trust me, that's not my intention."

"Trust me, that's not my intention," she mimed in a baby voice. "What the hell does that mean? You need to get your head out of your ass and realize you're living in a fantasy, Jay. You think that wife of yours is going to stick by you if you lose everything? No. When your shit hits the fan, she's going to walk away. I'm the only person on this earth who will love you through hell and high water." She stopped talking when she realized she'd said too much. The silence on the other end made her want to throw up. She knew exactly what was coming next.

"I did what you asked, but from here on out, we're through. Anything that needs to be discussed will have to go through our lawyers or Keisha. You decide, but you and me have nothing to talk about. And for the record, you need to clear that history out of your mind. You kept my son from me. You lied and told the world he was your baby brother. That's not my doing. I didn't make the record company pull your deal, or the movie producers refuse to work with you. You created this mess on your own. None of this has anything to do with me, or Christopher. From here on out, you can cancel the blame game. You are responsible for you."

She'd never heard him be so cruel. It was almost as if he was some kind ventriloquist dummy. He'd never talked to her this way before.

"Wait a minute, Jay, you don't mean any of this."

"We're through," he said again, maybe for the third time. *We're through.* The words rang in her head. But he wasn't finished destroying her. "No more using each other to get what we want."

"You think that's what this is about? I was using you? Jay, you are so blind."

"No. You're blind if you think there's anything else to our relationship. I'm out, CiCi. We're done here. Like I said, if you need to get in contact with me, call Keisha."

The swell of rage seemed to make her face burn hot all over again. She checked the mirror and she was right, the splotches she'd worked so well to cover were now lit up like red lights on a Christmas tree. Even the whites of her eyes were red. She wanted to drive a stake through his heart. No, they were hardly through. She wanted him to suffer unimaginable pain and she knew exactly how to do it.

Boxed Set

Ironically, I hadn't spoken to my mother since she'd left my house. With our only communication coming from the awkward translation of my father who wasn't big on using his words, the furthest we'd gotten was, say you're sorry first. I was angry. She was disgusted. We could agree on nothing except, "it wasn't *my* fault." Both of us had made this claim and were sticking to it.

By the fifth call, I'd decided to just say it, whether I meant it or not. "Dad, tell mom I apologize for not being more thoughtful of her feelings." My goal was to get past it so I could talk to my father about Bliss, and her connection with Grandma Sadie. Let's face it, my father was a locked vault unless my mother gave him permission to speak freely. He would never defy her and go down that road without her expressed okay. After all these years, my father was still beholden to Pauletta Bernadine Johnston. I couldn't blame him. If I had to live with her, I'd be afraid too.

"Dad, I want to see Grandma Sadie. At the very least, speak to her. I need to know how to contact her."

His silence was an indication he'd at least give it some thought.

I looked up while I held the phone and stared into the camera lens that was pointed at me. I decided I would carry out my day like Darcie, and the six other people standing around, weren't there.

"Precious, I think that's only going to make your mother more angry."

"Guess what, I really don't care. She's my grandmother and you and mom denied me a chance to spend time with her."

"I'm sorry about all of this."

"If you're sorry, make it up to me by giving me her information. Dad, it's time."

The phone sounded like it fell from his hand and tumbled before landing into my mother's. However, I knew that she'd probably snatched it from him. "Listen to me, young lady, you have disrespected me for the last time. Why in the world would you want to see or talk to her after I told you how she treated me? I am your mother. I gave you everything this world could offer. I carried you in my womb, I changed your diapers, and wiped your snotty nose. Have you no loyalty?"

I shook my head, "I don't want to keep having this same argument with you, mom. I guess I'll find Grandma Sadie myself."

"You do that."

The silence in the room was only momentary. I could feel Darcie gunning for some grand idea.

"How cool would that be? I smell a road trip to find grandma."

"I guess you haven't heard of a little invention called the Internet. I can probably search online and find her with some effort."

"That's even better. Once you know where she is, we'll go, do a surprise reunion kind of thing. It'll be a touching scene with her seeing her great grandbabies for the first time."

My instinct was to say No. Then I thought about it. "...seriously, do we have the budget?" I asked, thinking of Darcie's dedication to the dollar and contractual obligations. If they were willing to pay, I was going to give it serious consideration.

"Hell yeah. We'll get you to Mississippi, all of you. Jake, you, and the kids are going to see grandma to discover your roots."

The way roots stuck on her tongue made me want to gag.

"I'll check with Jake. He's not keen on the kids missing school."

"We can leave on a Thursday night, get back on late Sunday. Chris and My-my will only miss a day." She was impressed with herself.

"Yeah, okay. Like I said, it's up to Jake. Darcie," I said as pleasantly as possible. "Please do not shorten my children's names. I don't shorten them, so I'd like you to not do it."

"Whatever you say." She pushed the button in her ear where she'd obviously had her boss on speed dial. "I'll take care of everything."

I gave her a thumbs up. "You do that."

I headed to the basement of our house. I had my own plan that started with the boxes stacked ceiling high in the corner. Jake's boxes and mine from our separate lives. Mine were filled with old diaries, childhood mementos, and vinyl records from my favorite artists back then. Jake's boxes were filled with CD's of his favorite artists. That was really the only time I grappled with the difference between our ages of seven years. In that time, technology had sprung up and decimated an entire industry.

So much can happen when you're not paying attention. Time continued on without you. I sat on a stool after I'd pulled open the first box. I thumbed through the cards and letters, stuff I could never throw away. I had all the notes written in Spanish class with Mrs. Petra when I'd been trying to figure out how to say, I love you forever. It had taken over ten tries. The intended recipient, Milton Juarez, the boy with hair thicker than mine, had never read the notes. Turned out he was worse at Spanish than I was and couldn't make heads or tails of what I'd scribbled down. I was grateful I'd saved myself the embarrassment. Especially since he had eyes for another girl. Never did like competition, then or now.

In the bottom of the box was the envelope I'd hoped to find. My grandmother's big loopy handwriting addressed to me. I loved the way she called me Miss Venus Johnston. It was the last card I got from her. Grandma Sadie's return address was torn threw, but nothing a little tape and concentration couldn't fix. There was a yellow smiley face sticker next to my name. I'd torn the envelope haplessly to get at the crisp twenty-dollar bill I knew was inside. I probably hadn't even read the card. $20 was a whole lot of money for a kid and much too big of a distraction to be bothered with sentiments. The card was orange and yellow with a rainbow swirl of the number eight. "Granddaughter you're great and you're eight." An almost too familiar scent wafted up when I opened the card. "Wishing your Birthday is filled with rainbows and butterflies." Then beneath she'd signed, "Love you more than always, grandma."

I wondered if there'd been more cards and my mother just stopped giving them to me. How can you get cards from someone who has passed away? You can't. So of course, she would've pretended they'd never come.

I folded the envelope and took it with me upstairs. Just in time. I'd arrived to hear the commotion at the front door.

Enchanted Garden

"We're here to save you." Trevelle barged in with three other women each carrying a bible close to their chest. They were all dressed in white from head to toe like a band of angels. Trevelle poked her head in every direction before speaking again. "Are we rolling?"

Before I could answer, Darcie showed up with Shelly at her side. "Hello, good to see you all. I'm going to need signatures from everyone before we get started."

"Started for what?" I asked before remembering Trevelle's earlier visit. Spirits. Demons. "Oh," I sighed. "Whatever it was has left the building." Bliss had gone. My mother left shortly after. Unless the negative spirit resided in me, the house should've been good and clear.

Trevelle batted her long lashes and turned up her regal chin. "Let me be the judge of that. These are members of my Divine Holy Bible group. There's power in prayer. We'll find that nasty culprit and cast it out." She directed the ladies to sign their forms.

I faced Darcie. "You knew about this?"

"Of course. If I left sequences up to you, all we'd be doing is watching you nurse those little ones." She patted her mouth in a yawn. Maybe Darcie was the evil spirit. I hadn't considered it before, but it was more than plausible.

Despite my desire to tell them all to leave I couldn't muster the energy. "Do whatever you want. I'm going upstairs to nurse the little ones." I smiled for Darcie and her camera.

"Okay, ladies," Darcie barked. "You're on. Do your thing."

They did so quickly and got right to work. "Come together. Hands." Trevelle ordered. They gathered in a small circle. "Be prepared, sisters. It's stronger than anything I've ever felt before."

"I really think you're going to come up empty handed on this one," I whispered to Trevelle.

She ignored me, probably figuring my observation meant buckus. How would I know if there were good or bad spirits? I wasn't the best judge of character these days. All I knew for sure was that my house had never felt emptier than when Bliss had left. From the hallways to the windows, there seemed to be a void no one could fill. Not even Darcie and her crew. There was Jake, Lauren, and Henry, Christopher and Mya, and yet, the house still felt silent and depleted of energy.

I changed my mind about going to nurse. I didn't want to miss anything. I climbed on the couch in the living room and started thumbing through a decorating magazine. I felt Darcie's eyes on my back but I refused to be a part of her ghost-hunting scene.

The women hummed with their eyes closed while Trevelle sang out her prayer. "We come to you humbled by your power to protect all of your children, Oh Lord. No

deed is too small or too large. Bless this house. Cast out the
evil and pain that hides under this roof. I ask that you
watch over the family in this home and protect them. Bless
them, Lord our Father In Heaven. Amen."

I closed my eyes to feel the prayer. I needed some healing. Within seconds I felt lighter, relaxed, only to have the
moment end abruptly when one of the women sang out in a
short burst startling me. The women moved in unison
leaning on one another. I squeezed myself in the middle for
a group hug.

"Okay, let's spread out, ladies." She held up her cell
phone that was acting as a walkie talkie. "If you feel the
presence, holler and we'll come running. There's force in
numbers."

I watched Darcie. She was incredibly proud of herself.
This was the kind of television moment that would keep
her employed. Only thing she was missing was thunder and
lightening, but she could always add that as a special effect
later in editing.

She and her camera crew followed slowly behind Trevelle. Trevelle lifted her arms and closed her eyes as if she'd
felt something, then broke again in small steps. Every few
feet she'd toss a sprinkle of holy water from her little
bottle.

"So, it's gone right?" I asked when Trevelle finally made
her rounds and ended back in the living room.

"Not necessarily gone. The presence could still be hiding. But yes, it seems to have retreated," Trevelle had
assessed with a solemn expression. She'd come looking for

a fight. Nothing like a battle between good and evil to get the old juices flowing, but to her further disappointment there was no excitement. No flying demons to cast back to hell.

Perhaps it had been me all along, I surmised. Maybe I was carrying too much anger. I'd been trying to mask and suppress my misery under the guise of doing what was necessary to keep peace. A reality show. Accepting Sirena and Jake working together. When all along I was doing nothing but causing havoc in my subconscious. Either way, it was over now. I squeezed Trevelle's hand. "Thanks for coming anyway."

"This is for you." Trevelle held up another small clear bottle, this one tightly corked.

"Aww, a parting gift, how sweet. Thank you."

"This is no time for jokes, young lady. This here is some powerful stuff. Holy water is not to be used frivolously. Save it. Keep it close. If the evil returns, sprinkle it around you and your family."

I bristled picturing Jake, the children and I, huddled in fear depending on one ounce of blessed water to save us. "Okay. Thank you."

"Listen to me," Trevelle said. "You have to believe in something. I'd bet on God if I were you. What I felt here was no joke. And I'm telling you, whoever this spirit is has an axe to grind. You hear me?"

"I do. I promise to keep the water nearby and God even closer," I agreed genuinely. I thought about what Bliss had said, that our grandmother sent her to help and protect me. Against what? Myself. My inherently bad decision making. My new process would be to ask for a little guidance from the man upstairs. Pray first, decision later.

There was a calm peacefulness throughout the house after the women left. I packed the twins up for a walk. I couldn't think of a better way to finish off the day. The entire week had been traumatic.

I had almost made my great escape when I saw Darcie rounding the corner. Shelly was on her heels. "We've got to do this one over. You know I wouldn't ask because I know how you feel about this kind of thing, but we need to call in a professional. A real spirit hunter. Obviously your friend there doesn't have the gift she thinks she does." The pump had been primed. Darcie's dark brown eyes danced with flying spirits and Ouija boards. She wouldn't rest until she caught something amazing on tape.

"Darcie, I trust Trevelle. The place has a clean bill of health?"

"What I heard was that the spirit is hiding, not gone. We'll summon the spirit to come talk to you. Information is power I always say. We'll get someone to say a few things that only you would know. Get me?"

"No," I answered without hesitation. "I'm not going to start making stuff up, especially about something as serious as this. I've had my fill of spirits and exorcisms, thank you very much."

She shook her head in disgust. "I really don't understand you at all. Here you have this perfect opportunity to make gold out of geese's eggs, and you constantly are giving a thumbs down to every great idea. Why?"

"Because I'm tired, Darcie. I just want to go back to my life. Mine. Not the one you created for me and Jake."

"The one where you were barely paying your mortgage, that life?"

"Excuse me?" It took a moment to realize she'd stepped over the line. "Did you just speak to me about my personal finances, which are none of your business?" I took a peek down at Henry and Lauren comfortably strapped into their stroller. They were entranced with the toys wired across the top. I didn't mind talking about vagrant spirits, but calling Jake and I broke in front of my babies was darn right unforgiveable.

"Look, all I'm saying is that there are thousands of famous people out there that would jump at the chance to resurrect themselves with a show like this. You're taking it for granted. Believe me, once the lights go off, it's hella-hard to get them turned back on."

Hella-hard? Now she was using street slang, as if she needed to talk down to me so I'd understand. And after those nice ladies prayed away my bitterness. I took a deep breath to calm myself down. The whizzing noise in my ears had already started but I wasn't going to stand there and be pelted with insults. I didn't want to do this. I'd had enough drama with my mother and Bliss. "Darcie, I'm going to have to ask you to leave." I bent over one last time to make sure the straps were secure on the baby's stroller. I took a deep breath, grateful for the breeze. "All righty then. I'm off." I blew Darcie a kiss. "It's been a pleasure."

She in turn tapped her watch. "Your fifteen minutes is running out. Trust me."

I'd only taken a few steps but her words stopped me in my tracks. I did an about face. "Okay, Darcie, how about my fifteen minutes be over right now. You are not to step foot back in my house, do you understand. When I get back from my walk, you are not going to be here, do you understand?"

"We have the right to film until 8 pm. Its only 2 o'clock."

"No. You're not hearing me. I want you gone for good."

"I don't think that's what you mean. Especially considering you and your husband could be sued for breach of contract." She folded her arms over her chest as if she refused be moved.

I stared at her a beat too long honestly surveying which part of her to grab first. I pictured the entire scene in three seconds or less. Unfortunately that scene included a trip in a police cruiser. "Darcie, get your ass off my property." I said calmly.

She still did not budge. The camera was still rolling. I could hear the distinct sound of rage growing in my ear. She must've heard it too.

"Fine. But I will be submitting a bill for the crew's wasted hours today along with the expenses of travel and food, so far about six-grand. But trust me, this isn't over."

"I'll be sure to cut you a check." I rolled my eyes. I waited patiently while she gathered up her equipment and piled into her van. I raised my hand and did a middle finger salute when she and her crew finally drove off.

I felt better the minute they pulled out of the driveway. "Now, are momma's babies ready to go for a walk?" I peered into the stroller to see two sweet faces that reminded me of my purpose on this earth, which had nothing to do with a film crew. I inhaled the fresh air as we started down our path one happy step at a time. I pushed the stroller past the security gate where the guard was nowhere to be seen. Figured.

The stretch of road ahead looked endless. To make matters even scarier there seemed to be an incline. For some reason I'd never noticed the hill when I walked with Bliss. So busy talking and listening.

At the top of what felt like a mountain, I stopped and took a swig from my water bottle. The sky was clear. Every direction could've been the inspiration for great art. The sun bounced off the metal roof of a church. A shimmering cross stood high and prominent offering hope. Churches were still building and growing strong. They were popping up in the strangest places. While people were losing their jobs and homes, the faith business was the only recession proof industry, that and reality shows. I tried not to regret the run-in with Darcie and, knowing how furious Jake would be, but what was said was a long time coming. I lifted my arms and took in the freedom of having my life back.

Dangerous Turns

The money from the show would be missed but somehow, things would work out, they always did. I was serious about down sizing. We didn't need the colossal home and cars. All we needed was each other. I closed my eyes and said a short prayer. There was a reason the faith business was fail proof. Nothing else could solve problems in an instant but the belief that there was a brighter side and God would fix it.

I checked on Lauren and Henry who seemed to be enjoying the sky view as much as me. We began moving again. I was grateful the next few blocks were going down instead of continuing up the proverbial hill. My leg muscles were mush from pushing the stroller like a mule on a hot summer's day. I got as far as the corner before I heard a car coming from behind and made sure to scoot as far over on the road as possible without falling into a drain ditch. I never understood the South and their dislike of sidewalks.

I slowed my pace and waited for the car to pass but it never did. I glanced over my shoulder and saw a big SUV with darkened windows slowly trailing behind. I inched over a bit more. The car still wouldn't pass. After a few more impatient steps, I decided to ignore the driver who was obviously lost. They'd simply have to go around my double deluxe stroller and me.

Eventually, I stopped and turned around, this time ready to flag the driver ahead or ask if they needed directions but the SUV stopped too. It sat idling in the middle of the street with no destination. That's when my heart began to skip all over the place. I was being followed. Paparazzi was my first thought. Better yet, my first hope. Choices of who it could be were endless, sending my mind racing down scary paths. Stalkers. Fans. Baby stealers. I didn't know who it was or why they were trailing me. All I knew for sure was that I was in a terrible predicament. I couldn't run. I could barely push the baby's stroller at a decent speed.

You know in your gut when there's trouble up ahead. I saw myself doing high kicks and karate chops to protect Henry and Lauren. But deep down, I was a big scare-d cat. I told myself to keep it together. I whipped out my cell phone. I could call the police. But what would I tell them? A car was following me. I was an expert at calling the police, which meant I also knew the only thing that would bring them running was the possibility of a fatal injury, in other words, threats without potential blood in the streets and they were a no show.

After a second thought or two, I held up the phone to take a picture, aiming it directly at the vehicle's license plate. The driver wasted no time gunning the engine. The SUV made a difficult U-turn and took off on a speedy getaway.

I checked the picture. The license plate was too blurry. At least I'd scared whoever it was away. I took a couple of calming breaths and told myself it was no big deal. However-er, I wasn't taking any chances. I turned around and headed back to the house. It wasn't like me to turn tail and run. But I had more than myself to think about. "Sorry, babies. Our walk has to be cut short."

After a few seconds the thought occurred, what if the SUV was sitting over the ridge laying in wait. I dialed Jake's number. He didn't pick up. I dialed Gema next. She'd been thrilled when I told her I was taking the twins for a walk and she'd have the afternoon to herself. I figured she might be in the house giving her feet a much needed pedicure or sipping on green tea. Her voicemail picked up. "Gema, if you're there, could you hop in the car and pick us up. I'm about half a mile away toward the tree groves. And please be on the look out. There's a dark gray SUV circling the area."

I forced myself to move. I felt like Dorothy in the Wiz taking one step at time, envisioning lions, tigers, and bears, oh my. One step at a time and I'd be home, I kept telling myself.

Eventually I saw the security gate come into view. A new burst of power filled my limbs and I rushed the guard shack. As I approached I saw the security guard's head poached into his folded arms where he slept at his desk.

"Hey," I gave the glass a knuckle tap causing him to jump, nearly falling out of his chair. "Did you happen to see a dark gray SUV? A visitor? Has anyone come asking to see Venus or Jake Parson?"

He rubbed the sleep out of his eyes. "Man or woman?"

"I don't know. I just know the kind of car they were driving. What's that clipboard for? Don't you make visitors sign in?"

The nap hadn't done him any good. He yawned. "The clipboard, yeah. Let me see. A gray SUV is pretty common. I don't remember letting anyone enter in particular. Nope, nothing written on here."

"I bet. Thank you," *very little*, I wanted to say out loud. But I kept quiet and moved cautiously, looking in every direction as I began the last stretch of road to my house. "They just don't know who they're messing with is all," I muttered under my breath. Cause, mama, don't play. Sweat poured down my armpits and the crevice of my breast.

I entered the house and nearly collapsed. My knees were wobbly with fear. The house was quiet. "Anybody home?" I called out. There it was again, that emptiness. The void. "Gema?"

I unbuckled the twins and struggled to carry them up the stairs, one in my back harness the other in the front. I always felt like a mule when I used the very necessary apparatus. "Gema," I called out again with an exhaustive breath. I paused at the top of the stairs to get it together.

I heard movement. The noise was coming from the room Bliss had used. The door was closed but it was definitely a rubbing sound. More like swishing, as if a window had been left open and the curtains were flapping. Of course the wind had been too gentle when I'd been walking, leaving me a hot mess. I pushed the moisture of sweat away from my forehead before it dripped into my eyes.

My hand turned the doorknob. The air was cool but still had the scent I recognized as peaches, fruity and sweet, as if Bliss was still staying with us. Only then did I realize it was the same scent from my grandmother's card.

"Hello?" The window was open. The sheer fabric puffed in and out with the movement of the wind. I walked over to the window to close it. I glanced out and noticed a flock of birds dancing in formation. But on closer inspection they were butterflies. I'd never seen so many, except for the one time with Bliss. I stayed focused, almost mesmerized, watching them swoon over the wildflowers and circle the rose garden that kept blooming despite my neglect. I studied the fluttering wings until I couldn't see them anymore.

I locked the window and looked out once more and there below I saw someone. A shadow of movement. It was too quick to know, man or woman. I panicked and backed away from the window in case they were watching me. When I peeped again, there was no sight of anyone. Henry lifted his head, raising his big eyes as if to ask, what now mommy. My answer, "It's always something, little guy. Always something."

Wet Dreams

I saw the look in Jake's eyes the minute he entered our bedroom. Disappointment. Exhaustion. "What the hell happened? Keisha called furious. She said you cussed Darcie out and told her not to come back."

"I did no such thing. I mean I kicked her out, yes. But I only used one bad word. Technically for a cussing out, you need at least three words."

"Babe, I thought we agreed, three more weeks. Not even three whole weeks. Like two weeks and four days. Please, we have to do this." He pulled off his shirt and tossed it to the side. His bare chest was a sight for sore eyes, and anything else that ailed me.

"Darcie is the producer from hell. I'm not putting up with that attitude of hers."

"Funny, she said the same thing about you."

"You don't understand, this thing was killing me. Stress from having all those people in the house following me around. Listening to my every breath, I couldn't take it anymore." I squeezed my eyes shut and tried to muster the tears that could put it all into perspective. Nothing came but not from a lack of sincerity. Any other time, I could conjure up a few wet drops at a moment's notice, especially if it meant getting Jake see things my way. I probably had none to spare.

The afternoon had left me an emotional wreck. I'd cried out the trauma and confusion of the day while taking my shower. Everybody knows how good you feel after a long relieving cry. Unfortunately now I had nothing left.

"I think the stress came from having your mother here and your sister. You were fine before they showed up."

"That's not true. Darcie and her funky attitude were stressing me out, and if we add in Sirena, we've got a full case of crazy. I'm lucky I've handled it up to this point."

"Well, we're done with Sirena. I told her she'd have to figure out how to get her career back on track without me."

I clapped my hands. "Bravo. I'm impressed."

He ignored my patronizing tone. "Now. Impress me by—"

"I'm not apologizing to Darcie. She deserved everything I said to her."

"I already told Keisha to tell Darcie and the film crew they could come back tomorrow. You'll live through it," he said, adamant on not hearing any excuses. He leaned down and placed a solace kiss on my forehead. "Three weeks, babe. I know you can do this for me."

"This is all a big lie. We're nothing but an act. Nothing about this so called Reality is real."

"We're real. This family is real. Our bills are real. We've got two nannies, private schools, and six mouths to feed, and that doesn't include my mother's house in California." He left it at that before closing himself in the bathroom.

Bump In The Night

When Jake and I first met and fell in love, my mother was battling breast cancer and my then fiancé was being investigated for securities fraud, and possibly going to jail for a long time. With all that going on, Jake wasn't put off one bit. In fact, he relished in landing on my doorstep and making me feel better. Walks on the beach. Bubble baths. Foot massages. Whatever it took to ease my stress, he was there. When Mya was born, though he knew he wasn't the biological father, he held her lovingly against his chest for hours at a time just so I could get some sleep. He watched over me and did his best to smooth out my ruffled feathers, regardless of how deep my worries went. Our relationship fell into a guaranteed rhythm, I made trouble, he cleaned it up. A contract written in the sky.

But I feared he would grow weary of his role as the Bounty quicker, picker upper, ever ready to clean up my mess. That's why I never mentioned a single word about being followed by the SUV, or the shadow I thought I saw in the backyard. We endured enough with my mother and Bliss, then the whole Darcie thing.

After making love in the shower, we went straight to bed and held each other. He fell asleep while I listened to his light breathing. Keeping the information to myself was my way of giving him a break. Who wanted a spouse who had nothing good to say? Always reporting on tragedy and bad news? At some point you wanted a happy ending. I could barely remember one of those rare times when we shared conversation for hours, holding hands, walking on the boardwalk of the beach. Things seemed so easy when we laughed and talked about everything back then. We both preferred romantic comedies and hated horror flicks. The idea of sitting in a theater for two hours waiting to be frightened senseless wasn't either of our idea of a good time, no matter who came out alive. On one of those nights talking endlessly on the phone, we did the whole books, movies, and music comparison thing. He thought he was the only kid who was too afraid to see the *Exorcist*. Although by the time he'd been afraid, there was *Exorcist* 2 or 3 to contend with.

"Nope, there were two of us. Never saw it, never wanted to see it. Even the commercials that came on right when I was eating dinner scared the crap out of me." It was right before bed, going to sleep with a full stomach was the worst time of the evening to show heads spinning and little girls possessed by the devil. "I can't tell you how many nights I laid in bed scared out of my mind," I told him. "Once or twice I even imagined the bed was raised and shaking."

"See, that's why you need to spend the night with me and quit creeping out in the middle of the night," he'd said because I refused to wake up in his arms and do the walk of shame during daylight hours. "I can make all your bad dreams go away."

He proposed marriage in the chapel where we were attending my friend, Wendy's, renewal of her vows. I was already dressed as a bridesmaid with crystal earrings and a fitted champagne colored dress. He wore a suit with a crisp white shirt open at the collar. I stared down at the ring and blubbered like a big baby. Who was this man to change everything I'd come to believe about life and relationships? This man who'd slowed my pace and made me walk beside him instead of always in a hurry to get ahead.

I'd vowed we wouldn't end up like most of the couples I knew, distant or downright hostile to each other. We'd be that TV family who always wanted to know what the other was doing and have a kind word of encouragement. Who could've predicted we'd actually be the ones people were watching and depending on as the role models?

My family, prime time viewing. But if we were going to do it, I was determined to make sure we had family fairy tale instead of a tragic drama. I planned to find my grandmother and Bliss again and piece myself back together. Then I'd hold my mother's wigs hostage until she came willingly to my side of understanding. And my father, he would finally step up and assume his place at the head of the table. He'd laugh and be happy to have all his children and grandchildren by his side. It could happen.

I squeezed my eyes closed content with my wish and prayer.

But then I flashed them open. I held my breath to listen carefully not wanting any interruption in what I'd heard. What was that, and that? I snuggled against Jake's back and curled my knees under his body. I tried to put the subject of evil spirits hiding in the rafters out of my mind. Where was that holy water?

I held my breath for another brief pause and tried to concentrate on the sound I thought I heard. Footsteps. Adult size. Definitely floor creaking on the stairs. I knew that sound well. I'd listened for it many a time waiting for Jake to return home after his long tours promoting his movie or latest record.

I swallowed the heart shaking fear in my chest. "Baby, wake up. Did you hear that?"

"Hear what?" he asked with his eyes still shut.

"Someone's in the hallway."

He listened. Silence followed the way your cough has the nerve to disappear after finally getting in to see the doctor. "Wait. Don't fall back asleep. Just wait," I whispered.

We listened together. Nothing. Before long he fell back into a deep slumber.

For me, there was no possibility of sleep. Exhausted, yet, unable to rest my mind. Hallucinations. Faulty hearing. I accepted my state of delirium and continued to talk myself straight. The looming shadow across the room was not a person. The scratching noise outside the window was not an evil elf trying to get inside. She shaking and trembling of the bed was from my own erratic heartbeat.

The bump in the night is only my wild imagination, I tell myself again and again.

And then the loud thump. How do you avoid the sound of something falling, hitting the ground with a thud? "Baby, wake up?" *Okay, here I go. Can't say I didn't try.* "Maybe I should've told you earlier, but someone was following me today. Me and the twins when I took them for a walk."

"Sssh, I heard it," Jake said, instantly alert and climbing out of bed. "Wait here." He grabbed the bat I kept a hand reach away. My bat, leaving me defenseless. I slip on my robe and trail behind him. He tip toed to the babies' room and peeked in. When he pulled his head out the first thing he saw was me. "I thought I told you to wait," he chastised.

"Are they sleep? Everything okay?"

"They're sleep. Go. Back to the room," he ordered.

"No. I'm scared."

He took my hand once he knew it was a losing battle. "Okay, stay behind me."

Together we crept across the hall from one room to the next. We checked on Mya, then Christopher. Then one shivering step at a time, we took the stairs.

There it was. Right there on the third step...

"Did you hear that? That's the exact sound I heard. That means someone was up here. We should keep looking in the rooms upstairs, not down." I was proud of my super sleuth instincts. I didn't watch all those crime scene shows for nothing.

"Let me check the doors and windows first, make sure it's not just the house settling."

I gave him a solid elbow and whispered, "Stop pretending like you didn't hear what I heard. Somebody is already in here and you know it."

"Okay, okay." He did a turnabout and I followed him back up the stairs but not before the stair creaked again. He paused and stepped on it again. "Whoever it is could've been going up or down," he said in rebuttal.

"Fine. Let's split up. I'll check upstairs. But I'm taking this with me." I took a hold of my old pal, the bat, now in it's rightful owner's hands. This was as good a time as any to rekindle our relationship. We went way back. Been through a lot together. I gripped it tightly nearly covering the printed Willie May signature. I'd since upgraded. In the backseat of my car rested a small wrench that didn't require as much commitment. Swinging a bat took a lot of follow through to be effective. My wrench was small enough to pop someone if they tried reaching in to grab me. Trust me, I'd put a lot of thought into every possible scenario. But for now, my bat and me were back in business.

I peeked inside the bathroom, and the guestrooms one at time. I stopped when I heard bumping, like something heavy had been moved. The sound traveled through the walls. I closed the door and headed to the next guestroom with the same determination, bat held high ready to do damage. If someone was lurking around my house they deserved whatever they were going to get.

The noise was coming from the one Bliss stayed in. I'd closed the window from last time so I knew it wasn't from natural causes. I entered the darkness and was hit with her scent everywhere stronger than ever. It was sweet and fruity like a freshly opened pack of Now Or Laters. I wanted to step out of the room just to breathe.

I felt for the light switch. Up and down. It didn't come on. I listened and waited for the faintest sound while my eyes adjusted to the darkness. I took slow steps but still managed to stumble, twisting my ankle on something hard.

I checked back to see the culprit but the room was still too dark. I moved toward the window and pushed the curtain open enough to capture the moonlight from the sky. I caught a glimpse of what I'd tripped over. It took me three seconds or less to realize there were rocks aligned in a circle in the center of the room.

What tha hell! I scrambled towards the door and tried to turn the knob. It didn't budge. I screamed out. I tugged at the door.

"It's a circle of safety." The faint voice came without a face. Maybe if I opened my eyes, there'd be a face, but I wasn't taking a chance.

"Who's there?" I opened one eye at a time. "Bliss?"

"I'm here to warn you, Precious."

Precious was the name my grandma Sadie had started using when I was a child. In turn my father also used the name. It always made me feel so loved, yet here I was shaking with fear. My arms grew tired. The weight of the bat became too much and let it fall from my hands.

"I know what you don't understand is difficult to believe. You were always the stubborn one. Timothy would listen. Do as he was told, but you. No. You had to question everything and everybody." There was a slight chuckle but it sailed through the air like wind.

The words rang true of my grandmother. I was suddenly more afraid than ever. How was she talking to me when she wasn't there? I put my hands to my head. The ringing in my ears I'd been having now raised to a feverish pitch. It had to be Bliss pulling one of her magic tricks, maybe trying to get back at me. She was making all of this happen. "Why?" I said trembling. "Bliss, I'm sorry about everything, how my family behaved, but we don't have to let it interfere in our relationship."

"I love you. There's no need for you to fear those that love you," the voice replied. "I sent her here to protect you. I saw—"

Before she could finish, Jake entered the room. He flicked the switch and the light easily came on. "I was calling for you. What's going on?" His arms encased me. "You're shaking. What? Tell me?"

There's no one in the room except us. I pointed to the floor. There were no rocks in a circle, only the large wool rug with brown and gold swirls. I pushed my face deep against his chest. "I'm scared. I'm so scared."

"It's okay, babe. You're shaking. Come on. The house is clear. Let's get back to bed." He kissed me on the forehead and tried to calm me by rubbing my arms and back. But I was trembling uncontrollably.

"Not getting any sleep is making me crazy."

"Come on. Back to bed. I swear I'll hold you and won't let go," Jake said quietly.

I could probably count on one hand how many hours of sleep I'd had in the last month. I wanted that to be the answer for what I'd experienced. Whatever I thought I saw, and heard came from a place deep inside my subconscious.

It was the same thing after the stillbirth of our son. I swore I could hear him crying. I'd search the house, room to room, to find him. I never could figure out where the sound was coming from. It was so real. To the point I wasn't sure what part of my day was imagined or reality. I saw a therapist for nearly a year afterward. She made me understand how powerful the mind could be. We see with your mind not with your eyes. I wanted so badly for him to be alive. The combination of losing a child with the strain of post partum depression had been too much for me to handle.

I'll never forget that time. I was in a terribly low place. It couldn't be happening again. Not this time. Lauren and Henry were the joy of my life. Jake, Christopher, and Mya were my world. I had everything I could ask for. There were no pieces missing. No puzzles to solve. I just didn't understand why this was happening to me.

I must've eventually fallen asleep since I didn't remember Jake getting up from bed. The room was filled with sunlight. The night before felt like it happened a year ago. Hearing my grandmother and feeling Bliss in the room all products of my wild imagination came back as only scattered images.

I threw on my robe, relieved the frightful hallucination was all behind me. I was ready to take on the day. I attacked the stairs and landed hard, feeling a stabbing pain in my left ankle. I winced and touched the sore area.

Maybe I'd tripped on the rug. There were no rocks, I repeated. No circle of safety, really. I tightened my robe.

"Good morning," I said to Jake. He sat at the kitchen table with his laptop in front of him.

"Hey, how you doing this morning?" He got up and gave me a solid peck on the lips.

"Better. I think I slept. I mean really, slept."

"Yeah, you were knocked out. But you were still doing a lot of shaking and rumbling. Like you were running in your sleep."

"I don't remember anything. Guess that's a sign of a good night's sleep because I feel great," I said mildly fearful I'd jinx myself. I was ready for a new slate. I didn't want to harp on anything from the day before.

My focus was on getting healthy, mentally as well as physically. I wanted to challenge the onset of hysteria. I never wanted to be in the care of a therapist again. No mood stabilizers, sleep enhancers, there was no end to what a doctor would love to prescribe to fix the anxiety I'd suffered over the past couple of weeks. I swore to myself to let it go.

Darcie entered the kitchen. She'd already returned, setting up her make shift headquarters in what used to be Jake's downstairs office. "Good morning," she said with enough attitude to sound like she'd sneered her words.

"Hi Darcie. I wanted to apologize for losing my cool."

"No problem. I'm used to it," she said not bothering to acknowledge her role in the argument. "We have some catching up to do. I have a full list of activities I'd like to incorporate into your day to day scenes. Try to liven up what's left of our taping schedule."

I nodded. "Sure. Whatever you say." And I meant it. Resistance was futile. Like Jake said, 21 days. I could do it standing on my hands, or at least with my hands on my hips. Darcie would get no argument out of me.

"I'm proud of you, babe." Jake handed me a tall glass filled with his green elixir. "I added a little agave to make it sweet. I knew you wouldn't drink it regular."

"You're too good to me." I looked around the kitchen. "Does anyone else smell pancakes smothered with butter, syrup and bacon?"

The kitchen was spotless as I'd left it the night before, so it wasn't anything from yesterday.

"I have Bagels." Shelly held up a bag. "Your welcome to have one."

"No. I smelled a real breakfast. I guess, maybe it was coming from a neighbor's house."

"Someone's dreaming about food. Maybe there's another bun in the oven," Darcie said with a snicker.

I looked down at my stomach and knew without a shadow of a doubt that couldn't be true. What was left of me after the birth of Henry and Lauren did not include an oven in which to grow another bun. "Not likely," I said.

The doctor had warned that I probably couldn't survive another human growing inside of me. My blood pressure had dropped to a frightening level during the C-section. I'd lost too much blood. Our family was complete, Jake reassured me, as I lay in the hospital bed and signed the consent forms to close the oven for good.

"I should go check on the kids, make sure they're up and ready for school." I left Jake to go over the exciting activities planned by Darcie. My ankle creaked with pain as I climbed the stairs.

I knew where I was going but couldn't help it. I stood in front of the room after I'd told myself to leave it alone. I turned the knob, knowing I was making a huge mistake.

The door opened to the crisp morning sunlight. Stillness permeated the room and the floor was clear. Nothing was out of place. I breathed out a sigh of relief. No fruity scent. No giant rocks in the center of the floor.

I hummed the Temptations song, *just my imagination...running away with me* as I limped down the hallway to the children's wing. I peeked in to see Ursula standing officially over Christopher and Mya as they brushed their teeth.

"Good morning, you two. How are you?"

"Mommy," Mya nearly knocked me over rushing forward with a hug. I knew the feeling. At one point in time, there was just she and I, frolicking throughout our day. Quality mommy and daughter time uninterrupted. Now it was rare and almost reason to celebrate if we had more than an hour alone. I kneeled down and gave her a long rich hug. I went over to Christopher and wrapped my arms around him from behind. Seemed he'd grown an inch. His head was at my chin.

"Hi, mom," Christopher said. I'd never stop doing joy flips when he called me mom.

"Is Bliss coming back today, mommy?" Mya asked for the third or fourth time.

I finally faced her. "Not anytime soon, sweetie."

"But she was here last night. Why can't she come in the day time so we can play or have a tea party?"

"What do you mean, come in the day time?"

"She comes at night when I'm too sleepy to play. She reads to me though, and braids my hair."

It was as if all the air had been sucked out of the room. My heart thud against my chest. I stood up and tapped the area lightly as if I could kick start it on rhythm. "I need some water."

"Mrs. Venus, are you okay?"

"But aren't you going to comb my hair, mommy."

"Mya, come on sweetie, lets stay on schedule," Ursula said, rescuing me.

"Okay," she pouted. The toothpaste was running down the edges of her mouth.

"I'll do your hair after your dressed, baby." I gave her a soft pat on her head.

When I got outside I took a huge gasp for air feeling like the 500-pound elephant was not only in the room but sitting on my chest. I hunched forward and waited for the anxiety to pass. This must've been what Jake felt when he'd had asthma attacks in the past.

Eventually, the stream of gold dancing specks disappeared from in front of my eyes. The whizzing slowed in my ears. But the fear and confusion refused to go away.

Try Try Again

Bliss felt like a failure. She hadn't done what she was asked to do. The promise she should've never made in the first place had been broken. How was she going to convince someone as willful as her sister to believe her? Listening was one thing, understanding was something else.

"You should've tried the truth?"

"Grandmother, she would never have understood the truth." Bliss opened her eyes. She saw there was still a future. A chance. "There is still something I can do."

"Time is short. Do you understand? Make her listen and understand," her grandmother's voice was strong. Not like in real time where she'd barely had the use of her neck muscles.

Bliss closed the phone and pushed it back in her suitcase. She was late for her flight, but that didn't matter because she wasn't getting on the plane. She stepped out of the airport and waiting in the line for the next taxi.

Her heart was racing as she fought off the urge to do what she was capable of doing, soaring, lifting. Putting herself somewhere else took so much out of her. She remained where she stood on the curb but at least she was at the front of the line instead of the back.

"Next. Right here," the small man directing passengers extended a hand for her to get into the open back seat. "Where you headed, ma'am?"

She closed her eyes and saw the address. "31 West Avenue."

When she got inside the cab, the driver was eyeing her in the rearview. "That's the address of the hospital. Yeah, sure, but letting you know I don't take credit cards. It's upwards of fifty bucks, cash."

"Thank you. No problem," she said politely. But her mind was filled with harsh words. Could you mind your business and drive the car. If her skin had been fair with blue eyes the driver would've assumed she was capable of paying and wouldn't have wasted precious minutes with conversation. She needed to finish what she'd started. The guilt of knowing she'd only made matters worse, left her worried and angry. Tiring emotions. The foolishness of thinking with doubt drained her of energy. She hoped her sister wasn't rubbing off on her. Ambivalence was such a dirty word. It left a sour taste in her mouth. No. She'd never be that way. She knew exactly what she was going to do.

"So where you from?"

"All over," she answered before making a show of putting her pods in her ears. She refused to waste a single brain cell talking to him. Time was running short. Her grandmother was never wrong about her sight. What she saw nine times out of ten came true. It was ironic that she'd already come from a long line of women who'd harnessed their natural gifts into something powerful. She thought she'd have to hide who she was, and what she was capable of doing from her Grandma Sadie. Only to find out Grandma Sadie had lived the same way, hoping no one found out about her ability to see prophecies. It explained a lot. She'd been blessed with powers from both sides, her mother and father.

They were a match made in heaven. But then as her grandmother got older, the sightings were too much for her to bear. She was being hurt physically, as if she were experiencing everything first hand.

Like the time she saw the water rising to the point of waking up coughing up liquid. It was only a matter of days before the flood hit and washed out the entire neighboring city and Grandma Sadie was in turn battling a serious pneumonia infection. Or the time she couldn't stop smelling the scent of pine trees on fire. She saw the baby doll catch fire and woke up with burns on her hands. The story was on the news as Grandma Sadie sat in her chair trembling. She'd only been able to see the Christmas tree tumble as the little girl attempted to open her gift before anyone else was awake. A four year old and her parents died in the fire.

The last sighting was Venus. Grandma Sadie lay in her bed unable to move with blood dripping from her nose. It was the first time her grandmother had asked her to intervene. Venus had died in her vision. Though Bliss had agreed to try to save her, she hadn't really thought it possible. It was far easier seeing someone in a premonition of his or her fate than actually being able to stop it.

Her grandmother told her to feed her ground pistachio nut. Bliss nearly laughed. No, she did laugh. It was preposterous. Ground pistachio nut would save her life? Yes, Grandma Sadie had said through the telephone. Give it to her everyday.

"We're here," the driver shouted, expecting that she couldn't hear from the music pounding in her ears. He had no idea there was only silence. That was what she had craved on the long drive. She waited till he took her luggage out of the trunk, then handed him the fare, and not a penny more. Low expectations yielded low results.

"Have a nice day," Bliss said with a smile, though she already knew nothing nice would come for him. He was too angry.

The medical center was her destination. She wouldn't have looked so unusual pulling a suitcase behind her on wheels if she hadn't been wearing sandals and jeans. Otherwise she would've blended in as a pharmaceutical sales person. She stashed the suitcase in the rear of the building in between the dumpster and the brick wall. On second thought, there was nothing in the suitcase she needed. She had her money, and her phone in her pocket. She picked it up and heaved it into the dumpster all together.

She could still look like she belonged. Seeing the janitor's cart gave her the perfect alibi if she got caught. She began to push it towards the elevator. She knew no one would ask her a single question. Low man on the totem pole was always invisible. Even better now that it was lunchtime. The offices would be humming with relaxation. Dr. James was on the fourth floor.

The elevator door opened to the glass door of the waiting room. Bliss touched the door and stepped inside the over cooled space. The receptionist desk was empty. She marveled at the ease to just walk inside without a call button or security if any kind. A sign of good clientele she imagined. In the part of Little Rock where she'd grown up, everything was locked. Even the milk case at the corner grocer. She picked up the phone and dialed.

She cleared her throat and changed her voice, "Hello, I'm calling from Dr. James medical office. We have Venus Johnston scheduled for an appointment this afternoon at 2 o'clock for blood work. Just calling as a reminder. No need to call back to confirm. We'll see you soon." Even if Venus called back to confirm, everyone was at lunch.

She hung up with satisfaction. It would work. It had to work.

Fool Me Once

I checked the white pages online and a few paid searches and there was no phone number listed for my grandmother. I wanted to simply hop on a plane and find her myself. I knew it was rash but I'd been fooled once into believing she was gone, I didn't want to lose her twice without having seen her.

The next phone call was out of pure desperation. I didn't think Bliss would speak to me after the way I treated her. I used the number I was given when she'd first knocked on my door with her wild sister tales. I was grateful I hadn't sent her away no matter how bizarre things had gotten.

Before I pushed the dial button, a message appeared in my phone. The call came from my doctor's office. I'd forgotten Dr. James had asked me to schedule a check-up. I listened then looked quickly at the time. I didn't remember making the appointment, but I must have. I stood up and was immediately hit with the same dizziness I'd been experiencing. The lightheadedness had become so common that I'd gotten used to it, accepted it as the norm. And with all the chaos going on, I could've easily forgotten I'd made the appointment.

I grabbed a hold of the back of the chair and waited patiently for whizzing sound in my ears to go away. It always passed.

Except this time it took a little longer causing me to sit back down. I took a few deep breaths to relax. I knew that was the issue. Stress. The body eventually broke down after being abused with anxiety and sleepless nights.

I had some time. The drive to the doctor's office would only take a half an hour.

I picked up the phone and re-dialed Bliss. I could at least get some of the issues off my chest. I wanted to find my grandmother, and I wasn't going to be happy until I did.

The phone went to voicemail. I wasn't sure if it was the right number there was only the electronic voice as the greeting.

"Bliss, it's Venus. I know you probably aren't too happy with me right now. I wanted to apologize for the way things were left between us. Call me as soon as you can. I also want to talk to you about Grandma Sadie. I'd like to see her. I hope we can figure out a way to keep what we've found." I hung up, feeling like a scorned lover. I wanted her back and felt a bit desperate. But like any relationship worth saving, you had to put your heart on the line.

After giving it some more time, I stood up. I was fine, just as always. The whirling in my head went away. I rushed and got ready for my doctor's appointment. I kissed the babies and headed out the door.

As I was readying to get into my car it hit me again. But this time it was more like a striking pain in the back of my head. I reached out to balance myself. The car door seemed a million miles away. I felt a trickling of moisture down the back of my head. Maybe I hadn't rubbed the conditioner in my hair good enough. I touched the wetness and looked at my fingers. Instead of the shiny thickness, what I saw was red. Dark blood. I turned to look up assuming something had fallen on my head, and was met with a second strike. I went down without a pause hitting the garage concrete with a thud.

****

For a few seconds I thought I was dreaming. Blue sky and trees surrounded me, but the pain pulsing through my head was too real to be a dream. I lifted up on my elbows and saw that I was in the back of an SUV. What I'd been looking at was the sunroof and the large windows around me. This wasn't my car and I wasn't in my garage where I last remembered being. Fear shot through me and I fought the urge to scream for help. Who would hear me anyway out in the middle of nowhere?

I heard muffled voices, a man and a woman's. I peeked out the window and saw two people standing a good distance away. The man wore sunglasses and the trees shaded his face so I couldn't really make out any details on either of them. The lady was wearing jeans and a hoodie over a baseball cap. She and the man were arguing. He grabbed her arm and she yanked it away.

I ducked down. I searched around in the back of the SUV, hoping they'd taken my purse right along with me. She started toward the car. She was coming. Whatever these crazy people had planned was about to happen. I saw the keys dangling from the ignition and climbed to the front seat. I couldn't get the car to start.

Before she could get to the car a swarm of something came and circled over her head. She swatted and ducked. There were so many of them. They just kept coming. I turned the ignition and stepped on the gas. It took me a minute to realize, the car was in Drive. I pushed it into Park and tried again. When I looked up, one of the winged things was on the windshield. It was a butterfly. That's all, simply a butterfly right along with the hundreds of others that were keeping the crazy lady at bay.

I threw the car in Drive and pushed on the gas and accelerated.

I didn't get far before being trapped by trees in every direction. I jumped out and started running. I didn't know how close they were. I climbed up the shallow embankment and heard the sound of a highway.

I screamed, "Help me. Somebody, please." I climbed the rail and pushed myself over. I landed too close to the road. A car was speeding toward me but swerved and locked it's brakes before skidding to a stop. The force of air still knocked me off my feet. My head hit the pavement.

I heard the driver running toward me. "Stay down. I'm calling 911."

"My husband, call him. Distinguished Gentle..." I mumbled weakly before closing my eyes. It must've been enough to identify who I was or maybe someone recognized me. There was a benefit to being on TV every Sunday night.

My eyes fluttered open but I closed them back. The light was too bright in the room. I was in a hospital bed. Jake leaned over me.

He kissed my forehead. "You're awake. Can you hear me?" He stroked my hand. "Babe, can you hear me?"

"Ah-huh." My mouth was dry. My throat felt like I'd tried to swallow cotton balls and they got stuck.

A nurse came in shortly after. "Wonderful. She's awake. I'll get the doctor."

"Sweetie, what were you doing way on the other side of Dunne Park? You didn't have your purse, or car? What happened?"

I wished I knew. I closed my eyes and let the tear slide down my face. All I remembered were the butterflies.

"I'm just glad you're safe. You're here. God, I love you, baby. I love you so much." Jake rested his forehead on my hand.

The doctor came into the room. "Mr. Parson, I'm Doctor Nelson."

He leaned over me and flashed a blue light in each of my eyes. "We ran a MRI because of the blow you took to the back of your head. There was a lot of swelling. We wanted to rule out hemorrhaging, but what we found instead was just as dangerous."

Jake stood up but kept hold of my hand, preparing for the worst.

"Mr. Parson, your wife had a blood clot in her brain that could've erupted at any time. More than likely she had symptoms, but didn't know they were attributed to a blockage. If the clot dislodged, she could've suffered a stroke. If it remained in tact and continued to grow, it could've burst and led to fatal results. Either way, she's lucky. If she hadn't come in with a possible concussion, we may not have bothered to do an MRI."

Jake swayed side to side before taking the seat on the stool again. He took a couple of short quick breaths to try to get it together.

"We have her on a blood thinner. We're going to run another MRI in the morning and see if it the treatment dissolves it. Otherwise, she's going to have to undergo surgery."

"Brain surgery?" Jake's voice turned hollow. In fact, both he and the doctor were starting to sound like an echo funneling through a seashell. Waves rushing in and out to the ocean. They kept talking about solutions the way men do, but all I heard was that I could die.

The reality hit me like the blanket had already been pulled over my face. No. Please. I had babies to raise. I had important things to do. Jake saw the tears flowing down the side of my face. He leaned near my ear. "No, no, no.

You're going to be fine. You hear me, you're going to be just fine."

He blotted my face with tissue. More kisses on the forehead seemed to only make me more afraid.

"Maybe you should finish your discussion outside," the woman's voice came from near the door. I squinted past my tears and saw Bliss coming toward me. She took the place of Jake and leaned over me with a soft smile. The scent I knew so well wasn't overwhelming. It was calming. "You're going to be fine. Okay, the first thing you have to do is trust that you're going to be fine. You have to believe that."

For whatever reason, I understood. I nodded my head up and down, as painful as it was, to let her know I trusted her and believed what she'd said. I would be fine.

She left as quickly as she'd come. I watched her leave and focused on the tie dyed T-shirt she was wearing, yellow with purple and black butterfly wings stretched across her back. I knew right then and there all of it had been real. The safety circle had been real. It all made perfect sense in a world that made no sense at all. She was my butterfly, wings full of color and life. She'd been delivered to my doorstep by my grandmother to protect me.

Window To the Soul

Sirena kicked and scratched at her capturer. "Let go of me," she hissed.

"You know what, you're insane."

"And you're a coward. I can't believe I gave you money."

"You gave me more than that. Is it because I forgot to thank you, is that what's going on here?"

She squirmed under his grip. "Let me go."

"When you calm down."

"I'm calm," she squeaked out only because he was choking off her air.

"Okay then." He rose up slowly where he'd been straddled on top of her. She huffed and got to her feet. She dusted off the leaves and debris from the ground. He'd tackled her before she could catch up with Venus. Somehow she'd cut her hand and it was bleeding.

"You probably need stitches."

"Oh, go to hell. I don't want to hear your fake caring. If you cared about me, you would've done this thing so I wouldn't have had to. Now, I'm probably going to jail for the rest of my life."

"You're not," he said. "At least not if I can help it. I'll take you home, you can grab a few things. I'll put you on a plane. I know people who can make sure you're not found.

But you have to promise me you won't come back here and start this mess all over again."

"Oh, like you know people that were supposed to have done this job? I'm sorry, but your outsourcing skills suck."

He shook his head. "You're right. I should've ended this thing way earlier, but somewhere along the way I thought you'd have a change of mind."

"I kept asking, begging, you when...when was it going to happen. Did that sound like a change of mind?" She took off her hoodie and pulled the sleeve around her hand. It hurt like hell.

"I just assumed you felt something real."

It took her a moment but she finally got it. "Oh, you thought I was that into you." She gurgled a laugh in the back of her throat. "No, come on. You're a good romp, but sweetie, you're a hit guy. What kind of profession is that? Or should I call you Lucas. That's your name isn't it? Just a regular guy pretending to be something your not. I guess I should've known all along you were just playing me."

Again, he shook his head but this time he was gazing into the sky. He let his arms go up and down in defeat.

"I've worked too hard. I deserve better. And I want all my damn money back."

"As a matter of fact, I think you're going to get exactly what you deserve," he said still shaking his head in disbelief.

"But I'll take you up on that ride. Seeing as how my car got smashed into a tree, thank you very much. If you hadn't been wasting my time trying to talk me out of this, she wouldn't have gotten away."

"What in the hell were you going to do to her? Seriously? So you're a cold-blooded killer? Don't know how I missed that," he said dripping with sarcasm.

"Trust me, you have no idea what I'm capable of."

"Okay, I tried. Can't say I didn't try," he said to the air, the trees, the wasted space between them. "You can find your own way back since you like doing things your way." He turned and started walking. She followed him a short distance before thinking twice. She didn't trust him. Nothing worse than an untrustworthy man. She'd learned that lesson enough in her life.

She would find her way back to her house where she had a little cash, get her passport, and get the hell out of town. Once she was a good distance away, she'd figure the rest out.

She started the walk in the opposite direction that Lucas had traveled. She didn't want to run into him ever again in her life.

Eventually she came to an opening of the park and could see a highway in the distance. Someone would give her a ride. She walked on the edge. The first few cars hadn't bothered to stop. She could only imagine she looked a hot mess with her face splotched with redness and her sleeve soaked with blood. Finally the sound of a car slowing behind her. She turned around to see a police cruiser. "Shit," she murmured before waving. "Hello, my car broke down. Thanks for stopping. I cut myself trying to change the tire," she said all in one breath.

The officer walked toward her, then the second one got out of his car and reached for his gun. She stopped, breathless, scared to move.

"On your knees, ma'am."

She did as she was told. Her heart was pounding near her ears. "What's this about? I'm just trying to find a ride to take me back to my car.

"Sirena Lassiter, you're under arrest. You have the right to remain silent." She blurred out the rest of the noise. Her mind was already racing for an answer. She could say she was taken in the car too. She could say it was Lucas who'd taken she and Venus. She was a victim too. There was no proof of otherwise.

The officer led her to the back of the police car. She was helped inside and felt a pang of gratefulness to be sitting instead of still walking.

They started driving. Not more than a mile later they slowed down. Sirena looked up to see three or four squad cars and realized it was the area Venus had ran and jumped onto the highway before she could catch her.

The other officers waved them through. Sirena kept her eyes peeled for a woman's body splayed in the middle of the road. She could still wish, couldn't she? Instead what she saw made her chin drop. Better yet, it was who she saw that struck her dumbfounded. It was Lucas standing there talking with three officers. They'd found him. Good. "That's him, that's the man who took me," Sirena screamed out for good effect.

As the car approached closer, she saw something catch the light, a gold gleam hanging from his belt. "That's the man, why are they just talking to him. He's dangerous, he's got a gun," she shouted from behind the cage.

They ignored her. She quickly understood why. What she saw was a police badge displayed on his lean waist. She pushed back in the seat and closed her eyes. She didn't want to see him with a gloating smile of revenge. When she looked back, it was regret that shone on his face. He blinked true sadness before looking away. But it was her own remorse that made her tears fall.

****

The correctional officer tapped Sirena on the shoulder while she was having her dinner. White rice and liver with lumpy gravy. It was disgusting about a month ago, but now it tasted like steak. She turned around, "Yeah?"

"Warden wants to see you."

The rest of the ladies at the table clapped. "Hot date? You go, girl. Moving up in the world."

Sirena found herself inside a very well decorated office. Hardwood shiny floors and nice art hung on the walls.

"Have a seat."

It was a welcome treat to fall into the leather sofa. The door opened and Marsha Jackson entered. She was a petite woman with too much hair. It made Sirena miss hers. But extensions weren't allowed, one more rule on the list of many.

"Miss Lassiter, good to see you."

Sirena nodded. She wondered what this was about. She'd only met the Warden once when she was first brought in. Warden Jackson felt it necessary to explain the rules personally as if she hadn't been read the riot act at every level of entry.

This is not your personal dance hall. You will follow the rules like everyone else. Your fame means nothing here. Yeah, what else was new?

Warden Jackson picked up the remote and pushed the power button to her CD player. The music started and Sirena instantly perked up. "Wait a minute, where'd you get that?"

"It was sent to you, but as you know we check all media before it's passed onto the inmate. The entire staff has been singing this little jingle all day." She pressed for it to stop, then the eject button. She handed the CD to Sirena. "You're a very talented woman. I hope you see the error of your ways so that we can get you out of here and back to doing what you love."

Sirena took the CD. "Did it come with a case, a note, anything?"

"Yes, right here," Warden Jackson said remembering where she'd put it. "Here you go."

"Thank you," Sirena nodded. She left knowing better than to say more. Too many words never benefited anyone. It only would make her look weak. She swiped the budding tears before they fell visible to anyone. Inside her cell, she put the CD in her player. She opened the note written by Keisha. "Jake got the record to be released as a single. We started an account for you with a fifty-fifty split. The money will be waiting when you get out. We are all praying for you."

Sirena had never really believed in anyone or anything besides herself. But now she could feel those prayers working. She was going to have another hit. She and Jay did it, like she knew they could. They were the dream team. No one would ever be able to tell her differently.

Long Way Home

It took me a couple of months to feel completely good as new. Luckily I didn't have to undergo surgery. The medication did its job and dissolved the blood clot. I couldn't have been more relieved. Each day I felt better than the day before. The sad part was I had to stop nursing since I would be on medication for the next couple of months. Lauren and Henry didn't take it nearly as bad as I did. The advantage was that I could hold them at the same time with each of their bottles. We rocked gently in the large oak chair. Henry on the left, Lauren on the right snuggled close in my arms.

The doctors assumed the clot originated during their birth. I'd been a heavy bleeder during the cesarean and had been given a coagulation drug to thicken and slow the blood. The thought of not being there for raise my babies made me bristle with fear. Then I remembered fear never solved anything. I closed my eyes and whispered the words Bliss had taught me, may you be well. I said it continuously over and over and within seconds I demolished the fear.

I had so much to be thankful for. Even when the detective came for my statement, I could not find the energy to be angry or vengeful. If not for the attack by Sirena I would've never been in the hospital and gotten the necessary test. I knew it was a strange way to feel after what she'd done. But I understood the parts that made the whole picture. Everything led to the fact that I'd survived and come out stronger in the end.

"Babe, you ready?" Jake came into the nursery. He leaned over and kissed Henry on the forehead. "You guys ready to go for a ride?" Henry held onto his bottle with one hand and sent a chubby finger up to Jake's chin to let him know he could count him in.

"You sure this is a good idea?" I checked Jake's face for the answer that would tell me far more than his words.

He had a calm half smile. His dark lashes brushed against my cheek. "This is going to be a fun adventure. We talked about it. Besides it's only a nine-hour drive. We'll be fine."

It was the reassurance I was looking for. Georgia to Arkansas was considered a short haul, but we planned to take our time and spread it out over two days. We had the hotels mapped out down to each and every bathroom break. Maybe a bit over planned to be called an adventure, but when traveling with infants and children, it was better to be safe than extremely sorry. Mya was too much of a princess to do her business on the side of the road, that much I knew.

Once we got packed into the car and moving I became nervous and excited. Headed to see my grandmother and I had no idea what I was going to find when I got there. I pictured Grandma Sadie standing at the door with open arms, her house filled with life and something cooking on the stove. But, honestly, I was afraid. Bliss made a statement that gave me a hint that all was not perfect. Be prepared, was all she'd said. She gave me the address but nothing else. No phone number to call and break the ice. Only the promise that they would be expecting me and would wait.

****

We pulled up the address and I wanted to cry. It was a house, but it wasn't my grandmother's home. Not the one I remembered. The sign posted in the yard read, Gentle Care. It was an elder home facility. The white plantation style house was pleasant enough, but I just wanted to cry.

Jake reached around my shoulder and squeezed my neck. "We're here. We made it, thank God." He was speaking the truth. It had been a long trip. The twins got fussy after the second leg and kicked and screamed at the thought of going back into their car seats until eventually they cried themselves to sleep. I'd even suggested that we catch a plane back home. I wasn't cut out for land transportation.

"You think I should go in first, by myself?" Everyone had been traumatized enough with the drive, I didn't know what I was going to find inside.

"No," Jake shook his head. "We're all going in. It's going to be fine. We're a family. That's why we're here together. Keeping it one hundred." He gave a fist bump, letting me know, together, we could do anything.

We were a little beat up, but we filed out of the car and headed up the long paved walkway to the entrance. I knocked on the red-framed screen door and waited.

A woman in nurse's scrubs opened the door. "Hello, how are you? Who have we come to see this morning?" She asked with a vibrant wave of her hand. "Come in, don't be shy. Well look at these beautiful children. Oh my, just blessed. Marva, come look at this beautiful family," she called out.

Another woman came from around the corner with a towel in her hand as if she'd been cooking. "Yes, indeed. Welcome," she said brightly. "You're visiting today."

"Yes, my grandmother. Sadie, I mean Sarah Johnston."

"Oh, lovely. Follow me." The house was large. There were older people relaxing in various corners of the room, reading newspapers or books. Marva stopped and turned the book up the right way for a man who appeared to be really into what he was reading. "That might help, Dr. Francis. Make things a little more clear."

Christopher giggled. I turned and gave him a chastising eye. "What? That was funny," he grinned.

We ended up on the veranda with a huge white washed slat floor and white decorative iron tables and chairs sprinkled everywhere like a fine southern dining establishment. It was a picture from the past as if nothing had changed in fifty years or more but we still weren't there yet. Down the stairs and through a garden path we ended up in park like setting. There was a garden filled with roses and lilies. I saw Bliss and waved while still holding Lauren close to my chest.

I saw Grandma Sadie sitting in a wheelchair. I'd know her classic bun anywhere.

Bliss greeted me with a hug. We stayed like that for a long time. "I missed you."

She turned to grandma Sadie. "Grandmother, she's here. Venus is here," she said again slower.

"Grandma Sadie," I said, doing my best not to cry. "This is my family." She seemed to look right past me. She didn't respond.

"She goes in and out. Fourth stage dementia," Bliss said.

"But, I heard her on the phone, on your phone. That message. She was lucid and clear. That was only a couple of months ago."

Bliss put her head down. She took my hand. "I know. It's best that I explain later."

I knew better than to press her. Whatever she had to say probably wasn't for delicate ears.

I put my hand on Grandma Sadie's and she surprised me by grabbing mine back. "You have always been so stubborn," she said. "Just like your old grandma." I pushed my face against hers, so happy she recognized me. I inhaled her scent and remembered it was the shampoo. I loved that smell when I was growing up. As I kneeled, Lauren reached her arms around her neck too. Then just as quickly she began to stare out in the distance as if we weren't there. It was brief, but she saw me, she knew it was her willful granddaughter who always questioned everything before accepting its truth.

Later we took a walk and Bliss began to explain about the first time her phone rang and it was Grandma Sadie on the other end talking crisp and clear as if she were twenty years younger, and had all day to chat. "She didn't have any way to call me, she didn't have a phone in her room." We stopped and sat on a bench but could still see Grandma Sadie sitting in the shade with her Bible open in her lap.

"She didn't even know my phone number to ask someone to call for her and the nurses said it was none of them," Bliss continued. "I rushed here thinking a miracle had happened, and she was cured, but she was just sitting in her wheelchair staring out the window. I assumed I'd created it on my own. I wanted to hear her voice and feel her wisdom so bad that I created this way to talk to her. Then it happened again, and again to the point I was being driven mad. We'd have these long chats about her dreams and memories. Then I realized there always seemed to be truth in what she would tell me, like predictions, and these prophetic visions that would actually happen. Then the call came about you. She saw you on the ground with blood coming from your nose, a stroke maybe, she wasn't sure. But she wanted me to save you. She begged me. She'd never asked me to do anything before, to get involved so I knew it was important to her. That's how I landed on your doorstep, special delivery. Surprise, you have a sister."

It was too much to digest. But the easy answer was that she'd saved my life. "If you hadn't been there, Sirena would've succeeded in doing what she set out to do. It's just so weird how everything came in a circle."

"Isn't it? You never know how one thing is used to orchestrate another. You just never know." Bliss leaned her head against mine. "When I was little, and felt like a freak because I could feel things and do things with my mind, grandma Sadie used to tell me we all had gifts. Every one of us held power beyond our imagination, but most of us were too afraid to believe in ourselves. Too afraid of our own power." She faced me. "Don't be afraid of yours, sister."

"Mine?" I shook my head, "Listen, I'd be dangerous if I could do anything with my mind besides worry." I smiled, but I was serious.

"Don't underestimate yourself," she said.

"Well, look-a-here, we got more visitors for you, Miss Sadie," one of the nurse's called out leading a man down the garden path.

Bliss and I both looked up to see my father. "Dad."

"Like I said, don't underestimate your power," Bliss said looking over my shoulder.

I stood up and marched through the grass toward him. He was on his knees hugging his mother. Bliss followed.

He stood up and put his hand out to Bliss. She took a hold and didn't protest his hug. I knew one of those hugs could make everything all right.

****

Christopher was playing chess with Dr. Francis who was obviously better at the game than reading. "Time to go," I said.

"Aw, man. I'm winning."

"Let's go, buddy." Jake leaned over and made a move on the chest board.

"What'd you do that for? Now Dr. Francis has check-mate."

Jake grinned. "You have plenty of time to play chess and do all the things you want in this lifetime." Christopher got the message. He shook the older man's hand.

"Nice game."

We piled back into the car. My father and Bliss remained behind, waving as we drove away. They had some catching up to do. Turned out it was my father who'd asked Grandma Sadie to find Bliss. He'd been contacted by the social services when Bliss's mother had died in a car accident. She'd already been in foster care for a few months. He sent my grandmother to pick her up. He supported them both financially the entire time, all without my mother's knowledge.

I wasn't angry with my dad anymore. Just like that, I accepted the past and let it go. It was the passage grandma Sadie had highlighted in the Bible sitting in her lap. "This is why a man leaves his father and mother and bonds with his wife, and they become one flesh." My father did what he had to do to keep his family together. He'd taken on a wife, and regardless of how irrational that wife could be, he chose her. He'd made a mistake but wanted to keep his family and didn't know any other way to do it.

I reached out and held Jake's hand. I guess we all wished we had someone in our corner who would choose us first. I was thankful I had someone in my life that felt the same way.

CPSIA information can be obtained at www.ICGtesting.com
Printed in the USA
LVOW101058240513

335363LV00004B/198/P